About the Author

Colin Davies graduated from the North East Wales Institute of Higher Education (NEWI) Wrexham in 2001 with a BA Hons in History/English and worked for Tesco for 13 years until 2015. He enjoys reading, football and Formula One. He is married to Tina and has two young children, Jenson and Evie.

Dedication

I would like to thank Austin Macauley for their faith in this book.

Huge thanks to my parents for everything they've done for me.

And thank you, Tina, for your patience while I've worked on this.

This book is dedicated to Jenson and Evie who are my reason for being.

C. J. Davies

TALES FROM RIDGEDALE: THE GUARDIAN'S SWORD

AUSTIN MACAULEY
PUBLISHERS LTD.

A CIP catalogue record for this title is available from the British Library.

ISBN 9781785545108 (Paperback)
ISBN 9781785545115 (Hardback)
ISBN 9781785545122 (E-Book)

www.austinmacauley.com

First Published (2016)
Austin Macauley Publishers Ltd.
25 Canada Square
Canary Wharf
London
E14 5LQ

Tales from Ridgedale: The Guardian's Sword

When hope is thin in the darkest hour
Need will bring the Guardian's power
Faith endures not break or sour
Sword of fire and golden sand
Taken, but not lost from this land
Returned, a new King will finally stand

Chapter I: The End?

The Prince of Civitas Acerbus was known by many names; many of the titles bestowed upon him were not meant to flatter but he liked and used them anyway. The Evil Lord Pravus was most common, The Black Sorcerer was another title, Ater Veneficus or Dark Wizard were also used. Some knew him simply as Sinister.

He had ruled the barren lands of Pullus for close to five hundred years yet the Prince was no old man, much of that time had been spent preparing for the present. Expelled from the kingdom of Ridgedale and rejected by his noble family he settled in the dark wastes of Pullus after his failed attempt to seize the crown. His ambition to become king of Ridgedale had not dimmed, in fact it grew day by day, he ruled Pullus like a monarch, although in reality it was almost entirely populated by his Goblyn servants and most of the land was unpopulated save for his citadel.

His kingdom was a large Island just off the northwest of Ridgedale but though he ruled like one he would not allow himself to be called king just yet, not until the race of men would be defeated and bowing at his feet and he had the crown of Ridgedale on his brow. That time was now close, it was almost the moment to start the final grab for power. His contradicting emotions flowed wild within him, and he thought hard and often to keep them under control. He was impatient yet waited and planned carefully, his desire burned inside him.

As ruler of the barren lands of Pullus he had built a city appropriate to his power and the landscape, Civitas Acerbus was as black as pitch. It was known as a city but was little more than a fortress and it was surrounded by a great moat of dark green ooze. The centre of the citadel was a large dormant volcano which now served as his castle. The hollow caves inside made it a perfect base for his Goblyn army. Those who dwelt in the city were under the spell of Dark Prince for only a few served him willingly.

Pravus meddling in sorcery and dark magic had taught him one thing. He was good at it, excellent in fact, through this he had discovered the secret of long life, not immortality, but there would be time to learn about that after the war.

He dressed all in black, long flowing black robes, with ebony boots and gauntlets. The only exception was a chain like silver belt which carried his thin dark silver-grey sword and a slim silver crown which sat on his brow. His features could barely be seen hidden in the shadows of his attire. But his eyes were un-miss-able small sharp pupils in milky-white sea. A smile crept across his pale sullen face in anticipation of the future.

There was rarely a clear day in Pullus but on occasion you could see across the charcoal plains to the great river and then to the Silver City on the far bank. All these long years of draining his enemies resources was about to bear fruit, man no longer had the might to hold him back. Though he had waged war on Ridgedale for the best part of five hundred years the actual skirmishes were rare until recently. When battles were fought the outcome was unimportant only the aim, which was to weaken his enemies. He might take a peninsula or some other stretch of land knowing the Kings of Ridgedale would have to take it back. And sacrifice resources doing so. He also hoped that the fear of living next to him for so long would drain the will of his foes. It was inevitable he would one day soon launch all-out war.

In his service were men forced to his command by nefarious curses. They commanded his army of vicious Goblyns which had been growing for years. He also used Raptors to rule the sky; these vulture like birds could fire poisonous feathers from their wings, deadly to any prey. Soon his entire army would march across the river Evermore and sack Argentum the silver city and strongest outpost on the border.

Pravus had three trusted lieutenants at his bidding, the only ones who served him freely. He met them now in his throne room which was little more than a vast cave dominated by a large stone throne and massive stone table. Venom the Great Dragon, was fully convalesced from her near fatal defeat at the second battle of Skull Rock. During that battle almost one hundred years ago Pravus threw almost his entire might at Ridgedale but was defeated and the mighty old dragon seriously wounded. Venom had come to his service quite by accident, he was meddling with spells when one of them summoned the huge beast. All other dragons were thought to be extinct. Even the Dark Prince cowered briefly when the black wings descended on him but the promise of men to devour was enough to entice the creature to his cause. The dragon became his mark, all his forces Venom's likeness on their armour and shields. Venom had been lying low here for many a year building up her strength by killing the weaker Goblyns in sport, only the strongest troops went to war. Marauder was Pravus chief scout, he was a bitter and twisted man serving his Lord freely out of spite and hate. He was small and nimble and an excellent tracker, his dark green outfit made him almost invisible in the forests of Ridgewood where he spent most of his time intercepting messengers and spreading fear. He had become known in the woods as Creeping Death. Malice also served his Prince freely, he was an angry beast of a man who Pravus had made General of the Dark Forces. He struck an imposing figure which was bolstered even more by his armour which was shaped like bone right down to his helmet and mask which looked like a man's skull. Rumour had it that it was the skull of a King of old dug up to further intimidate opponents.

Sinister sat at the head of the long obsidian table; there were no other seats in the cave. He looked long at each of his lieutenants, as if reading their minds.

'We are ready all preparations are complete,' he let out in his rasping harsh voice at last. 'Go then.' With that the three nodded turned and left.

The sound of battle had been heard all week in Civitas Argentum the Silver City, Austin had almost become accustomed to it, almost. Austin lived in the Guardian Tower and he liked to think of it as his, he had lived in it all his life he was schooled here and it had almost everything he could want or need, it was his home but his father maintained it was the peoples, which in truth it was. The tower stood in a giant courtyard and was surrounded by a silver castle which the city was named after. The castle sat on a mound and dominated the centre of Argentum, at one time the city had a great moat around it but that had dried up years ago leaving a huge ditch in its place. The castle was a masterpiece stunning architecture, immensely imposing and beautiful at the same time; it was a tribute to the men who built it millennia ago, built to watch the kingdom's eastern border – which over looked the dark lands of Pullus. Many menacing gargoyles adorned the walls and fixtures of the castle and its tower, in the shape of dragons, trolls and ogres they were all painted silver. Argentum much like Civitas Aurum the other principal city in the country of Ridgedale were much alike in layout, though the Silver city was much older. Both were built around a castle and surrounded by a five meter thick wall roughly two miles in diameter and ten meters high. The Guardian tower stood the tallest of the castles five towers and Austin was often to be found on the balcony gazing into the distance. He was a good-looking boy fair of skin and hair, he stood a good size for his age. Standing on the massive balcony which offered panoramic views of the kingdom he could just make out the figures in the distance defending the kingdom in the name of the king, an old man who had never even set foot here. Did the he even care even care about them and the danger they constantly faced? It often seemed the king had forgotten about them. Austin reflected the war had been going on longer he had drawn breath, but this cold war was becoming increasingly hostile. The Lands of Pullus and the Kingdom of Ridgedale had fought for centuries on and off. But something had changed and everyone knew it and the whispers grew. Pravus real might would soon be revealed. The fight had already been taken to their side of the river, the enemy had seldom been as close as it was now.

Long had Austin's father Arian the Lord and Guardian of this great city held back the enemy as had his fathers before him. Many men had sacrificed their lives to protect the people of this land so many had paid the ultimate cost for freedom. But Austin feared his father no longer had the strength to hold back the enemy ranks by force and maybe even by will. Arian was also Guardian of the west and known as the Silver Knight and was Austin's only family, his mother had lost her struggle with a deadly fever when he was very young. His grandmother helped raise him but she had passed a few years prior.

Austin like many could only speculate on how the Evil Lord Pravus could keep throwing his dark forces at Argentum, it seemed he had more soldiers than there were waves in the sea. His father had never spoken of defeat, like his own father, his grandfather and many of his ancestors he had been tasked with maintaining the silver city. And as long as it stood it would always be on the front line, it would always neighbour the dread lands of Pullus. Only recently had Austin realised that the task of keeping the city would probably fall to him next, would he be strong enough? If the whispers came true would the city survive long enough for him to get the chance? Again he thought of the king and his army in his far off capital Aurum.

'Lost in thought again, young master?'

Austin turned to see his father's most trusted aide approaching him.

'I'm worried about father, Evan, I wonder how much longer he and the city can carry the weight of war.'

'He has called for you, it sounded urgent.' Evan was a wise old man formerly his Lord Arian's right hand man in arms. By odd chance he had lost his right arm up to the elbow in battle and was now tasked with tutoring the boy.

'Most likely I'm to be told off for being up here alone again, or for skipping lessons this morning.' Austin looked down to the city it seemed far below his tall tower; everything and everyone seemed so small so far away. He then looked across to where the battle raged, although it was a good mile away from the city wall from it seemed so close. Smoke drifted into the skies form several fires around the docks. It was uncomfortably close.

'I wonder why he's returned so soon from the front line?' he spoke almost to himself.

'Whatever the reason it must be important look there he is now' Evan pointed down at the figures racing through a gateway in the thick wall that surrounded the courtyard to their tower. Arian rode a magnificent grey stead and was clad in finest silver armour. Even blackened from dirt and battle they recognised him amongst the others. He pulled up and dismounted in one flowing motion and gazing above saw them waved smiled and proceeded quickly inside and out of sight.

'I was just thinking about him as you turned up, how did you know he was on his was back?'

'Word arrived early this morning I was told after morning study he would be back by noon, if you had shown up I would have told you sooner.' He smiled 'I have spent the morning looking for you should have known to check here first.'

'There's too much on my mind why bother filling my brain up with studying…'

'As your father always says life endures,' Evan interrupted, he had a kindly face but it looked far older than it was. 'You must get on with your life as normal as is possible, if we don't the enemy is on more step closer to his victory'

'I'm almost 17 Evan' Austin turned from the wall and started to walk slowly towards to door, his tutor followed, 'It won't be long till father calls me to battle.' He stopped and touched his elder's good arm and lowered his head. 'I'm not ready'

'Is that why you've been hiding up here all morning?' no reply so Evan continued 'I love the view from this balcony, while the view from back there might not be the most pleasant of sights, all we need do is move a few steps over here and the view becomes the mountains.' He dragged him around the balcony that circumvented their tower, Austin barely looked up. 'Looking south is the plains and then the sea but over to the east.'

'Is more mountains?' Austin sighed.

'So much more young master, the great forest and the river and if you keep going there's Civitas Aurum. Everything's a matter of perspective lad. Don't look to doom Austin, look to hope.' Austin turned his back and entered the tower. 'And there is hope and life that way you'll see.' Evan continued as they went down a flight of steps

'I've always enjoyed playing on that balcony. When I was smaller I would play wooden soldiers here, Pravus never won up here.' Austin stopped and looked at his tutor. 'There is no hope in the east as father would have us all believe, the Golden city has been silent for months, not a word from the King.' He now paced quickly down the remaining stairs to his father's study living Evan in his wake.

The study was in one of the towers smaller rooms, it had no windows just lamplight with which to see. In the room were two desks each barely visible, piled high with old documents and maps, next to the desks sat worn but comfy chairs. Although there were two desks in the room, one for the Lord Guardian of the Tower and the other for his son, Austin rarely used the room and in fact he only entered it when his father was with him. No one else was permitted in here, not even Evan. It was their personal sanctuary away from the rest of the world. The walls were covered various portraits of notable lords of the city and by dusty bookshelves containing hundreds of long since read old tomes. It was a circular cosy room, especially when the fireplace which sat opposite the doorway was lit.

Arian Lord of the Tower, Silver Knight and protector of the silver city entered his study put his sword on a desk and sat heavily in one of the chairs. He looked around the walls, he could trace his family back generations and all his male ancestors had served the city guard in some fashion, but it was his great great grandfather who was first to inherit the highest position in the city, and the most important, to lead the defence against Pravus and his dark forces. Abel was a modest cavalryman who stepped up to lead the cities forces after the great fire unleashed by Venom the dragon had destroyed most of the army during the Skull Rock conflict. Since then the lordship had passed to his son Aron and his grandson son Aiden both of whom served the city and defended the kingdom with distinction. Now Arian was in charge and it seemed the rule of the city might be taken from his hands. His father Aiden had come close to defeat more than once as Pravus forces had grown in strength in the recent past but had he always ultimately kept the enemy at bay. None of his family had sought the power and the responsibility of being the Silver Knight, yet they accepted it fate had thrust it upon them and they bore it with dignity. He was proud and that he was from a humble yet strong family, and it hurt that he now felt he was a knife-edge away from letting them all down. They idea of being the one to lose the city hurt Arian all those people who lived there would suffer and he knew many of them. But letting his father and grandfathers down hurt more. It was only a matter of time before the enemy's foothold on this side of the river was secured.

He looked at the fireplace on which stood pictures of his forefathers all holding the same magnificent silver sword, he took of his gloves and tapped that very sword sitting on his desk. It was a fine heirloom and a good weapon but his son would never use it. It was inscribed thus on the blade;

Only a hand in a glove of mail can hold onto the wyrm that bites its own tail

The sword's hilt was such that it had wrapped around it a slender razor sharp dragon motif and could only be held by Arian's gloves that had a tough custom made steel grip that fitted around the barbs. And even then you had to know where to hold the hilt correctly. The sword was presented to Abel when he took command of the tower. The Wyrm would never go to Austin though; Arian had a different future in mind for his son. A glance at a long dusty chest in the corner and then a heavy sigh. Yes he knew now what needed to be done.

There was a short knock at the heavy old door, then it opened slowly and Austin entered the room.

As he made himself comfortable Austin could see the concern, the worry, in his father's face. He knew his father had always done his best to be there for him despite the endless duties he had to perform and people who needed his time. He took great interest and encouraged his education and would also spend what free hours he had in this very room telling tales of strange beasts that lived in the forest and other excited tales, even stories of fearsome dragons. On Austin's fifteenth birthday Arian took him on a trip to Civitas Aurum, not by the direct route, known as The Long Road. Instead he took him through the great Ridgewood there and back; they camped and learned all about their surroundings and how to look after themselves in the wild. The expedition took over a month not including the three days spent in the capital, it was the longest time they had spent together in years and the greatest experience of his life. His father had changed a lot since then, and aged a lot too, his hair and beard had a lot more grey and rarely was he not exhausted. Austin spoke first

'You're well, father?' he asked and added, unsure of anything else to say at that moment, 'how goes the campaign?' Arian paused before answering and let out a big sigh that he tried to conceal.

'I can no longer keep the truth from you, son' he said in his quiet voice, 'the war goes badly for us; I'm concerned that our defences by the river will soon fail.'

'Surely that can't be true' gasped Austin.

'The Evil Ones ranks never seem to diminish no matter how hard we hit them, no matter how many times. They have started a push towards our lands and we have nothing left to push back with; our forces our depleted and strength is waning.' Austin opened his mouth to speak but his father held up is hand. 'Let me continue, son, I have something urgent to ask of you, a mission I can entrust only to you.'

'What can I do against such evil?' Austin asked; his head was still reeling from the news. The whispers were indeed true.

'If the Goblyn hordes gain a strong foothold over the Evermoor then I fear the Tower may soon fall into our opponents hands. To protect our people the city is now to be evacuated all will head to the safety of Civitas Aurum, only the guards will remain. They will be joined by the forces retreating from the riverbank at nightfall here behind these great walls we will hold up The Black Sorcerer.'

'Do you want me to help the evacuation then father?' Arian didn't answer immediately he gazed at the floor for a moment then almost reluctantly spoke.

'I'm afraid I have an even tougher mission for you Austin, you must go to Aurum a different way, you will go through the Ridgewood the way we went on your birthday would probably be best.'

'The great forest but why? It'll add days to the journey' Austin was shocked by this.

'The journey may only take five days assuming you keep a good pace on the Long Road but that doesn't mean you will escape Pravus and his Dark Forces. The road is largely exposed, it's predictable and our best sources tell us that it is already under surveillance. The Dark Wizard may not attack a large convoy but I cannot risk it, I can't take the chance him finding what I have hidden my entire life. You must take it to Aurum another way. '

'Take what?' his son asked wondering what his father could be going on about.

'Do you recall an ancient prophecy I once told you about? The one about Custos Ferrum the Guardian's sword. They say it was forged with dragon fire and the same golden sand that laid the foundations of Civitas Aurum and that it's long since lost.'

'Every boy must know the tale,' replied Austin 'they say that Luca the first himself used to behead one hundred Noelud warriors. But isn't it just legend?'

Arian slowly got up and opened the long chest and pulled out a long bundle tightly wrapped up in blue cloth. Austin could just make out a faded red marking on the fabric it almost looked like an eagle or some other bird of prey. Arian continued 'We all know what swords mean to our people they are emblems of liberty and strength, they are symbols of power. A soldier's sword may be plain while a king's is ornate but the message of virtue and honour is the same.' He put the bundle in the table. 'The old prophecy tells us the Guardian's sword will return and its master will unite men behind it in their darkest hour.' The bundle was placed next to Arians sword on the desk it was clearly longer.

'Father Do you mean to say that ...' Austin's voice trailed off...

When hope is thin in the darkest hour
Need will bring the Guardian's power
Faith endures not break or sour
Sword of fire and golden sand
Taken but not lost from this land
Returned a new King will finally stand

'The keepers of the sword have hidden it for countless generations. The Guardian's sword was smuggled out of Civitas Aurum generations ago by knights and hidden on purpose in order for it to remain safe, and it could when the time was right return with its power. No records show how it ended up here, but the secret of its existence here has been passed from one Lord of the Tower to the next for many generations, no one else knows of its existence here – no one. Why it was taken from the Golden City and brought here has long since been forgotten to most, I can only speculate it was for this moment now, when hope has all but gone from our land.' Austin couldn't take his eyes of the bundle, Arian continued.

'The Guardian's sword once was set high above Luca's throne in front of a tapestry of The First himself. Anyone who came before the king knelt not only to their monarch but symbolically to the sword itself. Already a famous blade it was after all crafted by the Phoenix years before it was given to Luca, songs were already sung about it. New legends were attributed to the blade with Luca though and one was soon very much believed. The idea of the Sword returning to save Ridgedale in time of need was whispered by the Phoenix herself. Then around 25 years after Luca passed away a group of Knights known as the brotherhood of the sword took Custos Ferrum from the capital. They took advantage of the turmoil at the time, Krul had led an insurrection against Queen Ebru. The loss of the sword was seen as an omen for Krul who was ultimately stabbed in his sleep. The sword was smuggled out of Aurum in a cart, old and very secret documents say three carts left the capital at the same time only a secret few knew which had the blade. All the carts were accompanied by outriders, two were decoys although the men who drove them didn't know that or even what they carried. Knowing the sword was missing Krul had the brotherhood destroyed. Ultimately the Guardian's sword ended up in Argentum under the protection of the Lord of the Silver tower. Though I have desired to I have never even taken it from its wrappings; I only know what it looks like from the sketching on papers in this study. Have any of our ancestors seen it? Who was the last to hold it in their hand I cannot even guess?' He paused for a moment Austin didn't take his eyes off the desk. 'Of this, though, I have no doubt; when the sword is taken to Civitas Aurum a new king will be crowned upon its arrival. The Guardian's sword is not a myth it is fact, it is real. And it can turn the tide of this war into our favour.' Arian paused to let his son take in what he was telling him.

'Surely you don't mean for me to become...'

Her father quickly cut him off holding up his hands.

'The Constant King must leave his throne; of this I detail I have known for many years. He has allowed a complacency to enter the kingdom which has given confidence to our enemy. He has not made a stand against Pravus against the will and advice of many and there are no signs that indicate that policy will change, so change must now be forced.' Austin noticed his father said this reluctantly. 'I only hope I have not left it too long to reveal the Guardian's sword, now seems the bleakest time in our history though. Both of the king's sons would make worthy successors, I mean for you to take the sword to them and the council. I wouldn't trust anyone else to take it please do this for me.' Austin seemed almost relived, he had struggled with the thought of commanding a city ruling a kingdom was not even a possibility.

'If I present them the sword will they topple the king though?' he asked. Arian could only shrug.

'In all honesty I can't tell you what will happen, but I firmly believe some change will occur when this sword is brought to Aurum. Please trust me on that. The sword is powerful beyond our comprehension.'

'But why can't it be you who takes the crown, who leads the kingdom? I can think of no one more suited no one who has led our city and its people better. You're the hero of the Tower, Argentum looks up to you.'

'Precisely why I cannot leave,' Arian looked sombre, 'and I have no desire to be a monarch and my place and home is here and while the sword will create a new king it will not be me. You must take the sword and I'm afraid you must avoid the open road so it can't go with the convoy leaving here, any sword may be dangerous in the wrong man's grasp, this one especially so.'

'What do you mean?' asked Austin

'Beyond it being a weapon not just any man can be king, my son, it has to be your destiny. The heirs to the throne were born to rule, taking the sword to them will be like opening a stale hut on a windy day. My gut feeling is that it will be giving the crown a breath of fresh air which the kingdom so badly needs. But it's not for me to decide who the new king will be either; the prophecy just teaches us one will be crowned. If the sword deems the princes unworthy someone else will reveal themselves. I have no doubts in this after studying the lore of the sword all these years.'

'You mean for me to leave soon don't you?' But Austin already knew the answer. Arian nodded.

'Pack your things. I will not tell you what to take I trust you know to travel light. I do have a couple of items you may want though.'

'Do you really think I can do this?'

'I know it seems hard son and that I'm asking a great deal of you but remember the biggest journey starts with the smallest step.'

Austin sat there for a moment then slowly went to leave the study but he stopped and gave his father a big hug before leaving the room. He could barely take all this in, his father wanted him to risk his live to carry an heirloom to Aurum. The alternative was to stay here and prey the city survives the continuing and growing threat. Either choice was dangerous. He trusted his father, trusted his judgement and trusted his teachings. When he spoke of the city and its fate his father seemed unsure but when speaking of the sword and the mission there was no doubt he was certain it was the right course of action.

Austin had never really pushed himself he was content just to not let his father down, he never gave his all at anything just did what was needed. Many former tutors told him he could be exceptional if he just applied himself, he was content to coast though, unsure on where his path, when he finally chose it, might take him. But Austin now sensed a determination inside that he had not felt before, if The Guardian's sword was to get to Aurum, he was going to do everything he could to see that it did.

Back in his room he packed a small satchel as many spare clothes as would fit, he threw his bow and a quiver of arrows over his shoulder, put a hunting knife in his belt and returned to the study. He knocked and entered the study before waiting for a reply. Sitting in the chairs he and his father had sat in not ten minutes before sat two of the strangest looking creatures he had ever seen.

Chapter II: The Old King

The Ancient city of Civitas Aurum had ruled Ridgedale as its capital since the foundation of the nation five hundred and seventy-nine years ago. Its splendour and magnificence were in no doubt, Aurum lay in the east of the country on the plains of Luca so named after the great king who founded the kingdom and built the Golden castle. Much like in Civitas Argentum, Aurum's castle had many tall towers and was located right in the centre of the city. This city was flat and the castle did not need to stand on a mound to dominant the landscape, its sheer size was enough. It was built in white stone with gold sand and had golden trim. The gargoyles here were made of white stone and took the shape of unicorns winged horse's griffins and other mythical beasts. This golden city had great circular wall roughly two miles in diameter that ran through it; it was the edge of the old town, newer buildings had sprung up outside the wall to house its ever growing population.

Ridgedale itself was an island nation; making good time on horseback it would be possible to cross it in 11 days as the crow flies. In reality a great mountain range divided the nation in half, that and its many canyons, rivers and hills and these added days to crossing the kingdom. It was a fertile country green for the most part with many great forests and plains. A vast contrast to the smaller island of Pullus on its northwest border.

Leland, King of men has recently started his 120 year, 99 of them as ruler of Ridgedale, and many doubted he'll see it out. But they had also thought that for years. He is known, though never to his face as 'The Constant' for not one of his citizens have ever known another king, he has always ruled them. Leland had always been conservative ruler since his first few turbulent years when he first seized power; he claimed to be a descendant of Luca the First to solidify his case to be king. No one could ever confirm this but it wasn't beyond the realms of possibility either. After all The Constant was from one of Aurum's great families.

He ruled Aurum well had maintained the status quo and few of its citizens could complain, indeed the city prospered throughout his reign. His rule was not so welcome outside his city walls however; it often seemed he had abandoned his people out there. He hadn't left the great walls of Aurum in half a century had never inspected the new town outside them, it was years since he even been seen outside his castle. While his kingdom waged war against Pravus in the west he keeps news of troubles from his subjects in the east, indeed only a few know they are in a conflict at all.

He sat now on his throne in his great hall content to let his council take day to day care of the land. His councillors had gathered at a large table to his left and were busy doing their duty. Signing and stamping official looking papers that were thrust under their noses by stewards busy rushing around the table and to and from the room. They all looked busy apart from Silos the council leader who sat at the head of the table; he just surveyed the rest through his sharp eyes. He need not disturb them and unless his signature was required they would not disturb him. Yes Leland king of men was very content right now. He was dressed in an old and faded crimson robe which was barely seen at the shoulders because of his flowing grey hair and long beard. His golden crown sat not on his head but alone on a table to the left of the throne. He gestured for an aide who immediately placed a footstool in front of his throne; he rested his legs upon it and slouched back into the comfy pillows. If it was not for the high golden back his seat would easily have been mistaken for armchair. But he was king and if he wanted a comfy throne then why shouldn't he at his age he reasoned. And he needed some comforts now with his sons constantly at each other's throats, and then there was his health. One thing he couldn't hide from his subjects was his age and the general ailments of old age had finally ravaged his body.

The calm in the throne room was shattered when the giant door to the hall swung open with a boom and in strode his eldest son and heir Lachlan. As ever his son was anything but discreet as he strode up to his father wearing his red tunic covered with golden armour with a scarlet cloak flowing behind him. On the middle of his breast plate was a mountain peak underneath a crown surrounded by a chain, the symbol of Ridgedale. He wore the armour always for Lachlan was a warrior by nature he was known as 'The Colossus' a title he loved and often referred to himself as it. He was a mountain of a man and sported a neat beard that matched his short curled brown locks. He had no interest in running a kingdom from a throne like his father; his desire was to be like a King of old, a conqueror. Lachlan was hungry for war and blood and his father knew this.

'How is my firstborn today?' spoke the king in his quiet voice. Lachlan threw himself into a chair next to his father's throne and while it was not small it protested under his size.

'All is well enough, father,' his deep tone did not hide his boredom, 'nothing ever happens around here that I need worry about.'

'Which is the way I like it, why don't you organise another hunt? That'll keep you occupied. And where is your brother, he hasn't been in the hall for days?'

'I care not where he is, you know I seldom waste time on him.

'You should be looking to the future my son. Past the crown that'll one day sit on your brow. Who will wear it after

- 21 -

you? You need an heir, a son. Leuan has no children either and the chances of him getting any soon are slim. He is a loner and not an attractive man, especially when all the women in court can't look past you.'

'I don't want sprogs yet, father.' Lachlan moaned 'you didn't have any till long after you sat on the throne.'

'But these are different times, my son. I wasn't born to be king; I took the crown to save the nation from the tyrant king's dynasty. You were born to rule and must act accordingly, and that includes having an heir.'

'Let Leuan have the crown when I'm done then,' was Lachlan's response, 'after all he wants it. It eats him inside that I was born first.'

'From the day you were born the crown was destined for you and then your children, it isn't Leuan's destiny. You need a son or daughter.'

'Give it to one of the bastards that are rumoured to be around then.' The king grimaced at this.

'If there are rumours no one told me.' Leland had of course heard the rumours from Silos and he knew that his firstborn had an interest in some common women. When some of said women were rumoured to be pregnant he had Silos take care of things, he, the council leader, was good like that, and also very discreet. If Lachlan had his fun with more prominent ladies it would have been harder to hide, though Leland was sure it could be managed. Silos was very resourceful and loyal to his king and wouldn't let something like a little brat born from lust harm the kingdom.

His son put his hand on the king's and whispered while glancing at the councillors.

'Your grace, send me to Argentum it's time to meet the forces of Pravus head on, will you not listen to your messengers? The city cries for help.' Leland tapped his thumb on his lips and looked into the distance

'The reports are greatly exaggerated, my son,' he said coldly at last. 'And as first General of Aurum's Guard your place is here by your king's side.' The king spoke calmly but the Colossus jumped up and threw out his arms in disgust.

'I will rot here!' He boomed; a man of few words he stormed off as the concerned councillors watched him leave, but put their heads back down after a glance from their liege. Leland did not worry about his son, they had had this conversation many times, Lachlan had often asked to leave for the west but he would never disobey his father. The old king would not risk his son's life. No, let the men of the Civitas Argentum concern themselves with that awful business he thought. The only real worry he had right now was what would happen to his kingdom when Lachlan did inherit the crown.

The king's council widely knew that the Colossus would undoubtedly and very publicly take the fight to the Prince of Civitas Acerbus and to that end they favoured his younger brother Leuan 'The Conniving'. When their liege inevitably passed they had no desire to see what they had accomplished torn apart by conflict. Wars were costly things and the rich men of the council knew this. Silos the council leader was on his way now in the dark of night to meet with Leuan, they believed he shared their views and to that end they hoped and believed they could manipulate him. The difference between Lachlan and Leuan was night and day. The second born was slender and unimposing, he shared his father's grey hair even at his relatively young age. His eyes were cold as steel. Leuan wore a white shirt with flowing long sleeves over which he donned a sleeveless dark scarlet coat. It reached his feet and had six gold buttons from his chest and a golden trim. Silos knew he had to tread very carefully with Leuan, for while many knew he was ambitious the council also knew his mind was as cold and quick as his eyes. Pulling his strings would be very difficult. But they had to try.

'It must be a most grave matter if the leader of the ruling council seeks me out on in the middle of the night.' Above the grand entrance gate to the city Leuan sat on the stone wall and watched Silos approach. The council leader was gangly, skinny and tall with jet black hair. The wall was deserted the streets below quiet.

'There are many in the great hall who worry about your father and his succession. Something must be done about your brother, maybe it would be best for all if he never …' Leuan cut him off.

'What would you have me do, Silos? Kill him perhaps? That would please my father wouldn't it? He spoke slowly his voice quiet, 'He's still my flesh and blood; be aware that we may be hostile towards each other and while our opinions may differ I won't do anything to him whilst our beloved father lives. He knows I despise him and that I would be king in his stead but he won't harm me for now either. But when the constant dies, then gauntlet will be thrown down.'

'We need to start making plans, my Prince, preparing for when that time arrives.'

'I already have a plan. Your council may back me but the city guard are fully behind my brother, he is one of them. He is more than that even, he is the golden child of the golden city and the people love him.' He spoke these last words very slowly almost lost in thought, and then he turned and looked across the wall to the mountains far off in the west.

'The guard would not oppose the will of the council.' Silos said quickly and defiantly.

'They wouldn't take kindly to you killing one of their own; they would smell a rat and they would be right to.'

'Are you saying that you'll let Lachlan become king, you won't challenge him, is that what you really want?' The council leader challenged.

'Maybe it's just meant to be. I've gone over this in my mind many times, once he's king he'll charge off to Pullus and to his death and we'll encourage him to do so.' Leuan shot a wry smile at Silos, 'he'll take a fair few of your precious coffers with him, so he we need him to go fast. The trick will be to make him take his trusted guard with him, rather than the militia who we can more easily control.' He paused for a minute, Silos said nothing just looked around uneasy, Leuan looked back. 'Once they've left the city I'll be unopposed. Big brother will be killed that is a certainty and then I'll be King. King Leuan III has a good sound to it don't you think? Lachlan's will be the shortest reign of any monarch in centuries, rather apt after our father's lengthy tenure.' Silos could see the wheels of thought turning in the Princes eyes, 'The simple fact is to get what I want I have to let Lachlan have what he desires, and he will bring about his own end. You can start drawing up plans to make peace with the Dark Prince though, no matter what father says he is a threat. I feel if we cede land say up to the great Ridge Mountains he'll be willing to listen to us'

'Forgive me but are you willing to give up our land? That's almost a third of the realm, our taxes depend…'

'Do you want to engage in all-out war?'

This stopped Silos. 'You believe that will work my Prince? It's a great deal of land and citizens to lose. And is it wise to negotiate with Pravus? I'm not sure we could trust him. What of the Silver City?' Silos now realised trying to control Leuan was a mistake, but he had laid his cards on the table.

'Of course we can't trust him but Civitas Argentum is all but defeated already, and not even the Colossus will be in time to save it; we may need to cut our loses. Think how much coin your council will save no longer bankrolling the silver tower. There are many paths we need to explore right not all plans we make may be needed. The Dark One can't capture to whole kingdom, I doubt if even his forces can be stretched that far.'

'Can we take that chance?' Leuan didn't answer he just looked back to the mountains barely visible in the dark sky.

'I trust that this conversation will remain our secret, even from the council.' It was not a question. After a few moments he dismissed Silos with a gesture. Silos left wondering how the council would be able to rein Leuan in, but reluctantly he felt the prince may be right. Leuan remained above the gate for a while though staring out to the west while a cold wind started to whip around him. A great deal needed to be sacrificed to save his father's kingdom he realised, his brother a formidable city and many lives. It would be worth it though the ends would justify the means. He smiled to himself happy in that knowledge. Leuan didn't wasn't to be a warrior king like his older brother he just wanted the power.

The following morning The Colossus woke in his sparse quarters, this room was the only thing humble about the king's heir. Situated right above the Royal Guards barracks his chamber was occupied by his bed a basin and mirror and various suits of armour in the corner, as he wore little else. The only other thing in the room was a small portrait of his late mother on a small table by his bed. He hadn't slept well, angry with his father for denying his request to go to Argentum once again. He would never wish his father harm but at the same time couldn't wait to finally be king. No heir to the throne in record had had to wait as long as Lachlan such was the length of his father's reign. He appreciated his father had his way of doing things but when he became king – Lachlan thought – things would be run a little differently. Let the council take care of the things they needed to tend to; let him rule.

His got up and pulled on a small black shirt and pants that barely fit him along with a sturdy pair of black boots, no armour this morning, and he stomped down to the barracks. All there greeted him with a nod; he kept things informal in here. He paused only for a cup of water then marched out to the courtyard. He had just the thing in mind to take his anger out on. The cells were directly opposite the barracks in a large old stone building. Two guards barred the only door each holding a long spear across it. Seeing their prince approach they moved aside opened the gate and bowed. Lachlan nodded in return.

'Keep the door open,' he said on his way past.

The room inside was split in two by heavy metal bars running from floor to roof, five Goblyn's were locked up on the other side. A warden got up and greeted Lachlan. These prisoners were captured months ago on the Hazeldene, what they were doing they would not say. They had slimy dark green-brown skin, patches of lank black hair and large dark eyes. Their long pointy limbs twitched as Lachlan addressed them.

'Today you have the chance to take your freedom, vermin. The door behind me is open and it shall stay open, all you have to be pass me.' He looked over at the warden. 'Open the cell put your sword on the floor between me and them and leave.' The Goblyns looked puzzled and they glanced at each other but none moved as the warden did as ordered; he had seen this before. Lachlan continued almost yelling, 'let no man stop them if they pass the door, but see to it that they leave the city immediately.' The warden agreed and left the room. The Colossus looked back to see him leave and the Goblyns charged, the first he swotted off with such force he flew across the room slamming into the stone wall and fell stunned. The next he grabbed and put a headlock on with his left arm. The third picked up the blade and charged the Prince, he blocked the blow by grabbing the creature's wrist and twisting it violently whilst pulling him down. Its grip on the weapon released Lachlan smashed his knee into him and the Goblyn's neck clicked horribly as head flew back. The fourth he greeted with a stiff kick to the midriff and he, too, went down winded. He wrenched the neck of the

Goblyn still under his arm and again a snapping sound was heard. The fifth didn't approach him, so the Colossus stepped up and grabbed the frightened beast's neck picking him up before throwing him backwards hard into the metal bars. Three still drew breath, one three and five. He strode over to the dazed maggot heaped against the wall and slung him into his comrade by the cell. The other he stomped and crushed with a mighty boot on his way over to them. He charged the only two left alive and pummelled them with his huge fists which were now drenched in the thick black treacle-like Goblyn blood.

When he left the prison to go and clean-up he stopped in the courtyard and looked to the skies. Such a pity, he thought, seldom are the creatures found; now they all seem to be gathering in the west ready to make their move. The next time I face them it will have to be in battle.

If only father would give me the chance.

Chapter III: Strange Companions

Sat in Austin's chair in the study that he had sat in not half an hour before was a giant cat. Though this cat resembled a man it had the face of a Cheetah. It stood quickly and went to shake his hand. This large cat wore large dark knee-high boots and a sleeveless blue tunic that had a white furry collar and trim. Its body was covered in golden brown fur with many black spots here and there, and had dangerous looking black claws instead of nails. It had a tail which twitched unexpectedly behind it like it had a mind of its own. Keen amber eyes and sharp teeth were all Austin saw though. As they shook hands it introduced itself.

'I'm Chajak of the wild cats, your father and I have known each other for some time.' It had a soft feminine voice but Austin knew instantly that it, rather she, was a formidable character. She carried herself with a confidence that Austin saw also in his father. A gold circular earring hung from her left ear. Next the second creature introduced itself stepping from behind his father's desk, but whilst Chajak was a cat this was a bird. His feathered head was brown with a few streaks of grey and he had a gold beak shaded with black. Large pale orange eyes with large black pupils met Austin's own. He was broad, much bigger than his cat companion, larger than their father even and Arian was tall. He was dressed in crimson with silver lightweight armour; his shirt was sleeveless like his companion's. His brown feathered arms were long and led to feather like fingers.

'Greetings I am Hcur, of the great birds.' He bowed. 'And I'm at your service.'

'What do you mean?' asked Austin stunned. Their father answered.

'They will be your guides, companions on your dangerous expedition.'

'We know the forests well,' spoke Hcur, 'my people dwell past the old forest to the east, and Chajak's kin dwell further east still. You will be safe with us.'

'I thought you people were a myth?' said the boy.

'No we are an older race than yours, in these lands anyway.' Hcur spoke with a certainty and a gravitas you might expect from a learned scholar. His large eyes were fierce and determined yet they were tempered with knowledge and age.

'Neither of our folk have much to do with men anymore,' piped in Chajak 'not since men started hunting us to extinction many generations ago, or at least tried too.' Arian stepped in when Austin's face dropped.

'That's the past and we can't change it.' He looked at his son, 'Its true men hunted their kind in the past but this city has built relations with them now, my friends here are emissaries from their people to Argentum.'

'We may be ambassadors to you, Arian, but the king of men still shuns us, refuses to acknowledge our existence you yourself keep us away from sight when we are here.' Sneered Chajak.

'You know that is typical of Leland he fails to acknowledge your people like he fails to see times are changing and dangers are growing,' he replied. But times are changing, my son is returning the Guardian's sword to the golden city a new great king will be crowned and maybe then your people can come out of hiding. You both know the legend. It'll be a new dawn for all of us.'

'Then it is true you have the Guardian's sword?' Said Chajak 'I heard the Phoenix herself cleaved the heads off five dragons with that blade,' she paused 'Time will tell about the latter, my friend, as for the former, I have vowed to see you to Aurum, lad,' she said turning to Austin again.

'Forgive my friend's attitude, little one, she is young and by her very nature she's extremely quick tempered. But she is also as noble and loyal companion as I've come across in all my long travels,' Chajak just rolled her eyes at Hcur. 'We know your father and his fathers before him to be trustworthy and relations between our peoples have grown from that and will hopefully continue to grow with you. Arian keeps us informed on what the world of men is up to and whether we need to be concerned about it, but as you heard your king would rather ignore us at the moment, which in all honesty has suited us fine till now. We are concerned by the evil growing in the west though.'

'So you know of the Guardian's sword?' Austin asked them.

'Of course, who doesn't?' replied Hcur. 'We had no idea it was here, though, all this time and with Arian. You kept it hidden well, friend.' Arian just nodded a hint of a smile across his face.

'We will all dine together here in the study tonight and get to know each other.' He looked at his son, 'Your journey will begin in the early hours under cover of dark. I'll fetch us some food.' He turned and left the study. Austin tried to think of something to say, there were so many things running around his head. Only a few hours ago he was worried about going to war, now here he was about to flee the city with a mystical weapon and mythical creatures. Both of whom now seemed to be studying him intently.

'So might I ask where in the land are you from?' Austin finally summoned the courage to ask them both. 'And how have you kept your existence so secret?'

'We birds live in what you know as the forbidden canyon; we have a small city there called Eagles Aerie. We are secret because your king wants it that way. Many centuries ago we lived in harmony but as man's population grew they invaded and took our land. Centuries ago your kings cut all contact with us and forbade men to go near what little lands we were left with. Both our peoples have been in hiding since then and rarely do our paths cross anymore.

'So that's why it's called the forbidden canyon, father said an evil old witch lived there.'

'And isn't there a myth about a giant scorpion that haunts Crosstree Rock?' Laughed Chajak.

'Well yes that's what we're told,' Austin said.

'Actually it's a great pride of cats. It's where we pushed back to, our last refuge. Ultimately we had to arrange a settlement, if you like, with men. Our lands are forbidden to you people hence the scary tales that were created'

'So why are you allowed in our kingdom if we're not allowed in yours?' Austin wondered out loud. Both creatures gave out a laugh. Then the great bird sat forward.

'The quick answer is nowadays your people are forbidden for your own safety.' With that an uncomfortable silence entered the room broken only by Arian's return with their meal.

'Strictly speaking we're not allowed in your lands and are still banished, our being here is against the king's law, but as I said events in the west have bought us here and Arian has always made us welcome.'

'Ignoring them is nonsense,' Arian simply said. Austin looked for more explanation so he continued. 'We can learn so much from them and they could be strong partners against Pravus.' With that he shared out what food he had brought. Austin realised even while his father had taught him so much – he had so much more still to discover.

After supper they picked up their things and made final preparations for the journey; food was packed, the best maps The Lord of the Silver Tower could provide were pored over and folded away. Then Austin remembered something else.

'Father you said you had some things for me, did you mean my companions?' Arian raised his finger near his cheek.

'Well-remembered, I have two items I would like you to take also, they might well prove useful. First is this length of rope, it saved my life once the first time I went into battle.'

'I remember the story.'

'The Story?' asked Hcur.

'Austin can tell you on the journey, you'll need good stories to pass time on the road. I would also like you to take my silver gauntlets,' he slipped them off his forearms and handed them over. 'I've always considered them to be lucky, they were your great great grandfather's, he was given them when he took command of the tower.' He couldn't help but look at his sword while he said this; the Wyrm remained on his desk.

'They are beautiful,' said Chajak studying the gauntlets closely. They weren't heavy and had an ornate head of an Eagle engraved in them. 'Are they Phoenix silver?' asked Chajak staring at them with wonder evident in her eyes.

'The finest and strongest material ever made,' Arian replied. 'My great grandfather was given them by Apollo, greatest of eagles'

'A very generous gift, phoenix sliver is extremely rare, it's unbreakable and its value can't be measured. But if I can add a word of caution, Lord Arian, are you certain that this expedition is what you want?' asked Hcur. 'The journey will not be easy.'

Arian grabbed his son tight and gave him a big hug which Austin returned. 'You know why you're doing this?' he asked.

'Yes, father,' was the instant reply.

'And you completely understand why I'm not sending you with everyone else leaving the city?'

'Yes.'

'Then Hcur, my friend, the way forward is laid before you. I have absolute trust it's best for all.' He picked up his sword and then led them through the empty corridors of the castle to the courtyard where three horses were waiting. Chajak now had two swords across her back and two small knives on her belt. Hcur now wore a large shield shaped like a bird's wings in flight over his shoulders and strapped across that was a large mace. As far as Austin could see he carried no other weapon. Before entering the courtyard they donned long dark cloaks with hoods pulled up and wrapped scarves about them to conceal their faces. Before mounting the horses Austin gave his father one last embrace. Arian had further wrapped the Guardian's Sword in its leather hide and he secured it to Austin's saddle as best he could. He gave it a pat as he looked up at his son.

'Take good care of it, and look out for each other.'

'We'll be back before you know it,' Austin said trying to be positive. Chajak and Hcur just exchanged glances.

'Safe journey, my son, remember on the road to listen to your companions but follow your instincts, too. I love you.'

'I love you, too,' he replied. With that Hcur led his horse out of the courtyard followed by Chajak. Arian almost had to push Austin's steed to get him to follow. As he waved them off movement caught Austin's eye from the other side of the yard. As they exited through one gate he could see troops entering from another on the far side, the forces from the river had returned to make a last stand in the city. Arian gave one final wave as they passed from sight then turned and went to greet his troops.

It took the trio ten minutes to navigate the winding streets to the gates of the city, the deserted alleys and tall buildings had never looked so foreboding to Austin. It was quiet after the issue to leave the city had been ordered many folk had packed their bags and left immediately rather than wait for the host to leave late the next morning. The narrow cobbled streets and paved walkways almost looked white in the moonlight rather than the usual dirty grey. The tall timber houses seemed to lean menacingly over the pavement. He wondered as he rode past some stores and a spiritual house when he would set foot here again. Of the four giant arches that made gateways to the city, the Southeast gate was rarely used, the Northeast and Northwest gates being more popular with travellers and city folk being on the more widely used roads. Even so the watchman still opened it for the travellers no questions asked, he barely even looked up; it would be a different matter if they were trying to enter the city at this time of night, they would most likely be refused entry. This got him thinking as they trod the dirt path that led to the old forest.

'Hcur how did you and Chajak enter the city surely the watchmen would have stopped you?' The hawk gave a little chuckle before answering,

'You must surely know there are more ways in and out of the Argentum than its four gates? Hidden passageways used by smugglers secret doors used by your troops your father knows them all and told us of them.'

'The only other way I knew of was the tunnel leading from the tower I thought for a while we might use it though it would be too small for the horses.'

'And that is why we just strode out of the gate,' said Chajak 'if we were to enter the city at any time we would surely be asked to identify ourselves in these troubled times, but no one cares when you leave, why would they, everyone's leaving soon anyway!'

'As long as we bolt the door on the way out,' laughed Hcur. 'Now let's get to the cover of the trees as soon as we can.'

Marauder did not know what had brought him to the far side of the city wall at this late hour. His instinct had told him to be here so he obeyed it; he found it seldom steered him wrong. For many the journey from Pullus to the city walls of Civitas Argentum would not have gone unnoticed but Marauder had done it not only with great stealth but very quickly. He was a master of not being seen, in a crowded room no one would give him a second glance, and he had spent his life hiding in the background. He had the sharp eyes of a hunter and the hearing to match. He wasn't physically imposing and rarely got in to hand to hand combat if it could be helped but could handle himself well enough if necessary, he was a skilled hunter and an excellent marksman. He took no hesitation in taking a life usually from a safe distance but he was known to slit throats from the shadows when called for. This is how he got the name Creeping Death. He also had something that no one else in the kingdom had or even knew that he possessed – a crossbow that fired small metal quarrels very quickly and accurately at their target. This weapon along with his considerable skills made him a formidable foe.

He was born with the name Kaiden but hadn't used it since his teens, not since he and his cousin led a small rebellion against the King Leland. It was quickly crushed and he went into hiding were he learnt his skills.

His jet black horse was tied to a small tree hidden by bushes some forty or fifty yards on the long road which headed off northeast. He didn't want to leave the horse but he had ridden her hard to get here and had to let her rest. Slowly creeping easterly always in shadow a noise in the distance drew his attention. It was the gate and three riders cantered out, after a moment they picked up their pace and headed straight into the Ridgewood. Marauder knew the forest well; most of his skills were honed there. He also knew few people made their way through the forest nowadays and none at this hour.

In another life Malice, General of the Goblyn Army would have been king. His grandfather Kraig IV was once ruler of Ridgedale, but he was deposed by a young challenger by the name of Leland. Kaine as Malice used to be known, like his cousin Marauder was brought up hearing of his grandfather's and his father's hatred of the king, of how he was an impostor and one day they would have their revenge. The former king was never able to extract revenge and reclaim his seat and Leland remained in power. Nor could his father gather the might either physical or mental to challenge either. The hatred and bitterness bred into them remained while the cousins travelled the land and their fathers made ends meet with menial jobs here and there. Malice would finally take revenge, though, for his old man now past. First he had tried when he was a young man, only to be defeated and lucky to still be drawing breath; with his cousin he had fled. All these years later he was about to get a second crack. Another chance to redeem his grandfather. He cared not that people widely held the belief that Kraig was a tyrant. Malice felt wronged; he should have been brought up in luxury wanting for nothing; this bitterness fuelled his hatred.

Malice and Marauder were in the Skull Rock market looking for any opportunities that might avail themselves when Pravus found them. The Market being a regular gathering place for nefarious characters that might be selling or buying ill-gotten gains and where many a wicked plan was conceived. The Market exists at the Skull Rock because there is no law in that region not since the great battles there; men now believe it a cursed land. The Army of Ridgedale was too small in number and too stretched to patrol everywhere so this Rock just north of the Fields of Evermoor was abandoned and criminals thrived there. The Dark Sorcerer had learned of the cousins and their hatred of the king and enlisted them to help him with the promise of riches and land when the kingdom was his. Neither of them needed asking twice they were glad for a purpose after years of wondering and it was a purpose that suited them rather well.

It had now been many years since the General had set foot in Ridgedale. His giant wooden flagship was being tied to the dock in the distance he could see Argentum shining like a beacon in the dark night. Dozens more ships followed the Generals in and were also secured. Countless Goblyns poured from the vessels. Some lined up others dragged equipment off the boats. As he disembarked he shouted for a report from one of his troops, the wooden docks were battered, small fires smouldered here and there the troops from the city had torched them to delay the Goblyns' landing. The stone walls also showed the signs of years of battle. He had been on this ship for the best part of a week battling the forces defending the harbour; at last they had fled.

'The harbour's deserted, sir,' said a tall Goblyn, 'they have retreated behind the walls.'

'Right, maggot,' Malice had no love for Goblyns and called them all the rotten names he could think of, they were just fodder to him. 'Get all our forces on land as soon as possible; no slacking then we'll march to the city immediately, if the men of the city think they've bought themselves some time then we won't give them the chance to draw breath.' The tall Goblyn grunted gave a nod and started shouting at others in his foul Goblyn language as still more ships docked. Soon the dark forces ships had to rope themselves together there was no more room in the port, the army scrambled from ship to ship carting their heavy gear to get to land. Malice was a good leader of his army; he didn't have to like them to order them about, and while Goblyns are dim-witted they followed his orders well and quickly. The greatest strength of the Goblyn army was not its intelligence, but the strength of its soldiers and more importantly the vastness of their ranks.

Dawn was just breaking when the army was all on land and Malice gave the order to advance. The Goblyn army beat their clubs and other weapons on their shields with every step and he allowed himself a smile as he rode behind his raucous grey-green soldiers on his large black horse. The road echoed loudly as they marched.

'March, Scum, the city will soon be ours,' he shouted. Revenge starts here, he thought, but it won't end till we reach Civitas Aurum.

Chapter IV: The Ridgewood

Austin and his new friends headed due east into the forest the road was even for the most part in the earliest stages of the journey. The night sky was clear and the stars lit the way, the scenery climbed and fell the path twisted its way through but stayed largely flat finding the easiest route which was now heading south east and far below the great mountain range. They were the South Ridge Mountains and were getting closer on their right hand side, snow could be seen on their high peaks even the dark. Going through those mountains was the direct way to Aurum, but they stuck to their chosen and longer path underneath the great range. They made good time on this track and travelled a good distance from the Silver City. In the early hours of the morning Hcur told his companions to dismount. They had come across a small clearing in the old forest and they decided to rest while they could. The forest was dark now but the moonlight lit the clearing well enough; it was not a cold night so they decided no fire would be necessary. The trees were old and thick in this part of the wood, Austin was no expert on nature but he correctly guessed they were mostly old oaks. They settled down and had a small bite to eat once Chajak had deemed the clearing safe. As they rolled out their packs and settled down Austin asked the Bird a question as he looked at his gauntlets,

'Hcur tell me more about Phoenix silver?'

'Ah Phoenix silver I could go on for days about it and still do it no justice, the history of it and that of the birds go hand in hand, young one, so here's a little history lesson to put you to bed. The first of the great birds to evolve into this form was the mighty Phoenix, we know her as the Firebird and she was also our Guardian. She was also the finest silversmith who ever lived no one since has been able to match her craft. She could create anything out of her silver from your gauntlets to goblets, from rings to weapons. Her silver is almost indestructible it withstands all but the most violent force and it lasts, those gauntlets you wear could be a thousand years old yet look at them they still appear new. For these reasons it is incredibly valuable, people and not just men, will go to many lengths to obtain it.' With that Chajak gave a snort lit a small caramel coloured candle and placed it near her makeshift pillow, she then turned her back on them and promptly fell asleep. Austin's focus remained hard on Hcur, though, who now recited an old poem sung long ago in his home.

The silver she created the finest ever known
Such a thing to behold
But the real treasure was your grace
Your beauty and your touch
It is of these now we sing
It is these now we miss so very much

'No other has been able to recreate Phoenix silver or even anything like it. The cats desire it, and why wouldn't they? And many of the bird folk believe it's our birth right and will do anything to possess some, generations ago battles were fought over it. The silver is also increasingly rare most of those who have it keep it locked away out of sight better to keep it secret and safe than show it off and lose it, much of it is now hidden or forgotten and lost.'

'What should I do with these then?'

'Conceal them under your sleeves, few should notice, after all who looks at kids' wrists? I won't tell you to take them off they should be worn and worn with pride in my own view.' Austin felt slightly better for hearing that and also noticed the gauntlets were barely visible under his sleeves even though they were bulky pieces. He also noticed they seemed to fit rather snugly even though they were worn by his father who had considerably larger wrists. Hcur picked up on these thoughts,

'It has an almost magical quality doesn't it? And he left it at that while Austin took in this information. The wise old bird made himself comfy in his own makeshift bed then continued. 'There is one item of Phoenix silver that few know about, though they may have heard of the item itself. Most people don't put two and two together but what I know as Custos Ferrum and you call the Guardian's sword was made by the Firebird herself and is the finest example of her work,

'Really?' asked Austin.

'Yes; remarkably most forget she created it even though she is a part of its myth. Its known to us as the Phoenix sword, It was her greatest achievement and a large part of why so much faith is put into the swords legend is because many, me included, believe it wields the strength and will of the Phoenix herself.' Austin looked at the bundle which was close by; he pulled it closer still as he curled up. They all desired to see it, even Chajak's ears momentarily picked up, but she stayed curled up. Hcur seemed to sense that, too, as he also made himself even more comfy. 'Some say the Phoenix forged the blade when she was attacked and caught defenceless by a dragon. They tell that in her plight she pulled one of her tail feathers into the dragon's fire that strafed the ground around her, then she plunged it into the cool waters of the Goodyson were she crafted it into a sword. Nonsense of course but a fascinating myth. Now let's get some rest, tomorrow may be a long day.'

Austin was aware that he was the last to fall asleep; as he lay there under the stars with two creatures he barely knew thinking about the sword and his father and what they needed to accomplish all his doubts grew. Did anyone else know about the sword? he wondered, as he finally drifted off.

When he awoke the next morning Hcur was sitting by a small fire cooking breakfast, all that remained of Chajak was the candle she lit the night before. The grass was damp from the morning dew, the sky seemed clear the sun was not yet out it would probably be a good day for travelling.

'Don't worry she'll be back soon' said the bird as if he read Austin's mind, 'Cats will often wander off but she won't be too far. She likes to check the territory. And don't underestimate her loyalty' he added reading the boy's mind again.

'How did you and Chajak come to know my father?' he inquired.

'The simple answer is that our two peoples have always sent emissaries to yours, most often they weren't welcomed, and King Leland has never acknowledged our extended hands of friendship. But the world being as it is and with the threat always looming from Pullus we have always tried. The Guardians of the Silver tower have always maintained dialogue with our peoples, but never to anyone's knowledge have our peoples travelled together like this. This expedition is new ground for all of us.'

'How well do you know father then?' he now asked.

'Better than any other man, though in fairness I can count on one hand how many I've met. I believe it's the same with Jak, I call her that, we first met him not long before he took up position as Lord of Argentum. Your grandfather introduced us. Apart from sharing knowledge about Pravus and the dark lands, though, we have few other dealings.

After a small breakfast of cooked meat on toasted bread the pair packed up their belongings as Chajak reappeared.

'Morning, my friends, I've done a little scouting and our way seems clear for the next few hours at least,' she said while picking up her candle and packing it away in a rather small and barely noticeable shoulder bag.

'Good work let's be on our way then shall we?' Hcur motioned to the horses.

'Not yet.' Austin held out the sword in its wrappings. 'If our path is safe for the moment then I think it's time to see what we are carrying.' Chajak and Hcur looked at each other, but said nothing, and then the cat nodded and took a few steps towards, but stopped short of Austin. The wise old bird stayed by his horse. Austin knelt and put the long bundle on the short green grass, his hands trembled as he slowly removed the layers, and he looked up at the Cheetah and the Hawk and could see the anticipation in their eyes. Tension filled the clearing the air seemed heavier. Finally after what seemed like an age the sword came free of the cloth and he held it aloft. Time froze again as he pulled it free of its scabbard. The Guardian's sword attacked all his senses. He was struck by its size it was such a long sword how did it fit in those rags? It was so light it took no effort to hold it in front of him but there was a real weight to it. He could taste the scent of history on the weapon, but he could only guess at the number of warriors who had wielded it, no marks or blemishes showed its age though. But what caught his attention most of all was its beauty, its elegance, its simplicity. It was all silver no other colour not even on the hilt. The blade was thick yet didn't appear to be so, and it was inscribed with ancient markings, the Bird's tongue or maybe old runes he guessed. The hilt looked like bird wings going into the handle which was like a twisting column big enough for two hands to grip yet it could be held easily in one.

Silence held the group for a while whilst they admired what they saw. Austin finally spoke.

'It's stunning like no sword I've seen before.'

'It is a fine piece of craftsmanship no mistake,' agreed Chajak, her face burst into a huge smile showing her sharp teeth, 'imagine soon this weapon may bring the dark prince to his knees'

'All the more reason to get on with our journey,' added Hcur 'we have a mission let's see it done. Let's not get ahead of ourselves.' After Austin packed the sword back up he mounted his horse and the others did the same. He didn't say a word and the others watched him carefully as he trotted ahead.

Austin had felt odd since seeing the sword, it wasn't what he expected yet it was much more. He carried the future of the kingdom on his horse it was a great deal to take on board. He also missed his father this morning; he realised that while he could sometimes go days without seeing him, his father always knew where he was, now he was in the wilds and getting further away with every step. The woods cleared for a bit as they entered a glade. Chajak stopped her horse and looked around; sniffing – her eyes narrowed.

'Something isn't right here, Hcur, though I don't yet know what.'

'OK, my friend, we will press on with caution,' answered the Hawk. They rode on for a bit till the middle of the glade then without warning the horses plunged into a swamp that was hidden from view.

'This shouldn't be here this isn't right,' yelled Chajak as they backed their horses up.

'This wasn't here on the way down,' agreed Hcur. 'Swamps don't just appear from thin air some devilry creeps across the land before us.'

'What do you mean?' asked Austin scanning the area ahead with the others, not sure what to expect next.

'I don't like this at all,' hissed Chajak.

'We'll go round,' stated Hcur.

'I don't like it,' repeated the cat. Before Hcur could say anything else, though, trouble erupted. With a great rush a massive green beast burst up out of the waters, it was at least twice the size of the hawk, the biggest among them. It looked almost like a giant broad crocodile standing on its rear legs but with a shorter wider jaw and mean grin, the swamped dripped from it. The startled horses reared up and threw their riders, Hcur and Austin fell in to the swamp, Chajak's reflexes allowed her to backward roll off her steed's rear and land knee deep in the swamp on her feet, she quickly drew her swords. The beast lunged at Hcur and swatted him aside then turned to Austin, the Cheetah leapt on its back and it swotted her off, again she landed on her feet. Austin was wading out of the swamp as quick as he could holding the wrapped sword close to his chest, the beast grabbed him and flung him several feet back. He dropped the blade when tossed and his first thought was to retrieve it. He saw the sword a few feet away and desperately scrambled towards it. Hcur called out and the beast now turned to him, the Hawk, now armed, brought his mace up under the creature's chin. Swamp water flew from it and the weapon arched through the air before it made contact. A crack was heard and the beast cried out in pain, the mace had taken out some teeth. Chajak again leapt at the now bloodied creature landing on his shoulders she cut across the beast's throat. The monster fell backwards into the swamp from where it came, the cheetah jumping clear before it landed.

'Where's the sword, lad?' demanded Hcur.

'It's OK I've got it,' came a relieved reply. He had found it before it sank out of sight and once again clutched it close.

The whole attack lasted barely more than twenty seconds, but they were all breathless.

'We need to take even more precautions now.' Panted the Hcur. 'This can only be the work of the dark wizard. As he casts his gaze further to the east he causes mischief along the way.'

'Yesterday I thought your people were a legend today we are fighting swamp beasts. It's been a strange day,' mused Austin. 'I don't think anything else could surprise me on out journey now.'

'Don't be so sure, lad,' said Hcur with a quick shake of the head.

They managed to get their horses back but they had lost most of their food and their spare clothes were drenched also.

'Well we'll need some new supplies,' sighed Chajak. 'I wanted to avoid towns on our journey now it seems we will need to stop and replenish our packs.'

'Let us leave this place right away,' ordered Hcur 'we will discuss our plans when we are far from here and satisfied we are safe again.' Now they knew it was there they could just about make out the swamp's edges, they gave it a wide birth as they left the clearing and continued through the Ridgewood.

The next morning Chajak rode beside Austin for a bit casually chatting but not talking about much until she finally asked a serious question.

'What training do you have?'

'Training? What do you mean?'

'In how to take care of yourself out here? Can you look after yourself if need be? For example if the sorcerer somehow discovers our plan and makes a play for the sword?' The cat looked at Austin hard. He just shrugged,

'I know how to use a sword and I can fire a bow do you really think we will need to fight?'

'We did against that swamp beast didn't we?' the cat was silent for a few moments while Austin thought about this. 'I don't wish to patronise you, lad, but we may hit trouble again on this journey, it's a long trip and trouble may follow from the west, or maybe we'll happen across bandits in the woods, there are many of them, yours is a lawless and dangerous country outside the cities, the point is I want you to be prepared. Hcur is a mighty fighter but if trouble occurs we may not be able to fully keep our sharp eyes on you. Your father and I spoke a little before we left and with your permission I'd like to train you in a little of our defence skills while we are travelling. The cats are skilled warriors, and this invitation has not been extended to any of your race in my knowledge.'

How could he refuse an offer like that even if he wanted to, and it wouldn't hurt to be better able to defend himself. He didn't know what to do when the beast attacked them in the swamp his first thought was to flee while his friends drew weapons. No that wasn't true is first thought was the sword, then it was to run he realised.

'I'd be delighted if you would teach me anything,' he replied.

'Don't think it will be easy. Cats work hard for years to hone our skills and we all continually learn new things every day, it also helps that we are built quite agile and are quick on our feet. You will be learning on the road never easy to rest, but I'm glad you have agreed it heartens me and my hopes for the quest have been boosted. You're more like your father and less like other folk of your kind who seem less open minded in my view. We may yet achieve our task.' Austin noted that the cat spoke like she had little faith in them, could bandits or anything else really cause that much trouble out here? He prayed Pravus knew nothing of the

Guardian's sword; the idea of being chased by the Dark Forces did not appeal.

'The Sword must get to Aurum I have to do it, Chajak, it's what my father wanted I can't let him down,' the boy looked off into the distance.

'*We* won't. Lord Arian is a fine man and a credit to your race, will you follow in his paw prints when this is all over and the sword is in safe hands?'

'And rule Argentum? I don't know if I can, Chajak. I wouldn't know how.'

'We are friends now Austin, call me Jak. You are full of doubt understandable at your age.'

'I just wish I knew what to do, not just with this task but also…'

'You're hoping to find yourself on this trek perhaps?' the cat asked with a little laugh, 'maybe you will and maybe you'll be the champion who wields the sword against Pravus and lead us all to peace and prosperity?'

'Is that so hard to believe?' asked Austin liking the idea because someone else had voiced it. 'After all the sword was entrusted to me it might be my fate?'

'Was it not entrusted also to your father?'

'It was passed to me, which must mean something!'

'Let me tell you what I believe.' Chajak looked at Austin as they rode and reached over and put her hand on the boy's wrist. 'I don't think you can wonder out here and wait for fate to happen. Life isn't about finding yourself it's about creating yourself.' With that she gave Austin a big toothy grin and rode on ahead a bit as was her custom to scout the tracks they will soon tread.

From then on Jak trained Austin whenever they stopped, sometimes just for a few minutes sometimes for an hour or longer. At first the boy was taught some basic self-defence techniques drilled into him over and over. Often Hcur would add words of encouragement or advice when needed, and Austin appreciated the support after taking many a tumble and receiving a few bruises. After a while they moved on to using Austin's bow, he was a decent shot already but Jak improved his skill further. It was the fifth day in the Ridgewood and after a long trek walking in sodden rain Austin was in no mood to train. Taking cover from the constant downpour in a small cave he was ignoring Jak who was going over some instructions.

'Austin. Austin are you listening to me? What I'm saying may save your life one day.'

'Not now, Jak, I'm tired and soaked through,' protested the lad.

'We don't stop learning because were tired, boy, do you think war stops because the little boy hasn't had his catnap.'

'I'm not a soldier I just want to get some food and my head down for a bit, I can't even take it all in right now.' The cat stood over Austin.

'I'm doing this for you for your safety. Take out your bow.'

'I won't do any more now.'

'Get your bow,' she hissed.

'It's all too much!' he shouted back.

'Let me tell you something Austin I can accept failure.' She paused before she sat down. 'Everyone fails at something. But I won't accept not even trying. It was a mistake to think I could teach you.'

Hcur having lit a small fire now chimed in. 'Perhaps you're being hard on him my friend; remember he isn't like your kind. We could all use some rest now. He says he's tired and I believe him as I am myself. What can he learn about his bow now?'

'This is more than a lesson now old friend it's about a mind-set. It's not important you succeed but you have to try you know that and if he won't...'

'Your words are wise but you also know there is a right time or wrong even for everything.' Chajak looked at Hcur for a few moments then got up and left the cave. Passing Austin she said.

'The only people who never fail are those who never try.' He didn't look up as she strode out into the rain pulling her hood up and slipping from view.

'She's frustrated and tired herself, Austin, try not to take her words to heart.'

They waited for the rain to subside before continuing the next day. Jak hadn't said much when she returned; as they trotted on their horses Austin starting thinking more about his companions.

'Tell me some more about yourself and your people, Hcur.'

So while they travelled Hcur told tales of all kinds, Austin learned the Hawk liked to tell them and that he didn't mind repeating himself which he often did. He told Austin that while the great birds always kept themselves to the region around the Goodson Canyon and largely kept out of the way of the ever increasing habitats of man the Cats roamed the land and settled where they wanted. They soon found themselves under man's feet. Village's, towns then cities sprang up around them. All tolerated each other at first but as man's numbers continued to increase soon the cats and to an extent the birds were seen as savage. Hcur then explained that by the time Ridgedale was founded many Cats found themselves as slaves to men. At least the slaves were kept well, though the more unfortunate of them were reduced to begging in the streets for scraps. It was only a matter of time before trouble arose.

'That's terrible,' said Austin unsure of what else to say.

'The Birds had an age old friendship with the Great Cats and when they fought for their freedom we joined their cause. It wasn't so much a war as a rebellion but the old King Jaffroy agreed, being a learned man, to give the Island of Crosstree Rock to the cats to settle on, and the Canyon where our great Aerie sat he declared off limits to his people. He put no commands on our races save to govern ourselves responsibly, and the Cats have now grown strong and numerous since doing so.'

'Jaffroy? The old Jaffa, he is one of our greatest kings, but his reign was over four hundred years ago.'

'A long isolation indeed. Still we have maintained dialogue with people of your race mostly with the silver tower which I always found strange as it is the farthest city of man from the Aerie.

'The Aerie? You mentioned it a few times what is it?'

'The Eagles' Aerie is our capital, I look forward to you one day laying eyes upon it, for it is a remarkable place, but I will not say too much about the Aerie now I wouldn't want to spoil it for you. It sits in the canyon through which the powerful Goodyson flows. Being the inquisitive being I am I longed to see new lands like my kin of old so I became a scout then emissary to the silver tower when the chance allowed it.' The forest cleared for a stretch for the next few miles the Ridgewood and its great trees spread further south. It would soon return to their path in some five miles. Until then landscape was flat with short green grass. Elk could be seen in the distance Jak had already earlier mentioned they were that night's supper.

'So we are heading that way then, to the Aerie I mean?' Austin asked presently, 'it's not the most direct way to Aurum is it?'

'No it will add many a day to the expedition to be sure but we will need more supplies I'm sure and it's still best to avoid the obvious routes. Jak and I agree that the attack in the swamp was a sign our journey may not be going unnoticed. We also agree *our* races need to know of the sword as it re-emergence ultimately affects us all. So the Aerie will be a place where we can recharge ourselves after many days on the move. And we're still not sure what reception will await us in Aurum, young one.'

They rode in silence for a bit and Austin thought about all he had learned in the past few days. Some if it seemed so hard to take in. He realised it made sense to let Hcur people know about the sword and he was curious to see the Aerie and more of his guide's people. But his father hadn't mentioned going there and this nagged at him. *Follow your instincts.* His thoughts always went back to the sword though. It was so majestic could he part with it when the time came? Did he really have a choice? Already he felt an attachment to it. All he was certain of was that if he wasn't ready to follow his father's footsteps how could he claim the Phoenix's sword and become a king? Then a thought struck him about the great firebird herself.

'What happened to the Phoenix?' he asked Hcur. The bird surprised him when he started to sing softly,

Where is the firebird now?
Sought after for so long
One day with luck we may find out
Until then we sing our phoenix song

O wisest and greatest of birds
Immortal always to be reborn
Hidden from us for an age
And so we shall ever mourn

What made you take flight?
Why have you not returned?
Surely some peril must have befallen you
A fate we have not yet learned

Firebird there was only one of you
Unique in every way
Flaming red you were in hue
And piercing eyes of grey

The sword one of many
Yet unlike all the rest
Unto that sword you gave your strength
To await one final test

He paused for a bit after this ode as if in deep thought or maybe recalling a great loss. After a while he simply said.

'We don't know what happened to her.'

They rode on once more in silence for a bit that morning all seemingly pondering the journey they had undertaken. As in the previous day the land was terrain was flat and the path stayed mostly straight so the trio made good progress in that morning. The pasture became thicket for a while then they crossed three small brooks until they came to a meadow, Chajak noticed cows grazing in the distance and went to fill her canteen with milk, but there was no sign of anyone else much to Austin's relief. In fact he thought with the obvious exception of the swamp beast it was a pleasant journey was so far. He had learned so much.

'As were going to be depending on our horses for who knows how long I feel we should name them, what do you think?' asked Austin eventually he'd had been thinking of names for some time in truth.

'Name them?' questioned Hcur.

'Definitely, mine is grey and white with a wild look I'll call him Wolfe. What shall we call Jak's?'

'You'll name Chajak's horse for her?'

'Yep to save the charger from a silly name that she might think up.' The bird shook his head with what sounded like a little chuckle. 'Chajak's horse will be March because she's always marching off ahead off us what do you think?'

'I like that name; it seems very appropriate,' The Hawk agreed with a wry grin.

'That just leaves a name for your steed.'

'Ah well I have come up with one already, young sir.'

'Really?'

'Yes she'll be Ensign.'

'Where did you get that name from Hcur?' scoffed Austin who had already thought up the name Shadow for the black horse.

'Well I rather like the name and also it's imprinted right here on her reigns.' He laughed, as did Austin recognising the tanner's name embedded on the leather strap.

Up ahead Chajak had stopped not far from where they were to re-enter the forest, they saw she had signalled them to wait also. After a few moments she turned her horse back to face them they could all see her quick eyes studying the foliage, she would take the occasional deep breath through her nose. At length she gestured for the duo to join her and they rode up quickly.

'What do you smell my friend?' but Hcur sensed he knew the answer and he felt uneasy now too.

'Trouble,' was the reply from Jak. Austin gave both a worried glance. 'The wind has shifted now that it follows us

I've confirmed a scent.' The cat gave her companions a long look. 'We're being followed.'

Pravus looked out across his domain. The balcony carved into the rock high up in his volcano provided an excellent view of his city. Civitas Acerbus was deathly quiet now the last of his forces where marching towards the river. Word had got back that the silver city had already fallen. Malice and his Goblyn army had won the battle even before all of his troops had arrived. He knew they would. The first step on the road to victory. The rest of his troops would now strike out across Ridgedale from there. His ebony gauntlets gripped the balcony tight something was wrong though and he couldn't work out what that was. As powerful a sorcerer as he was he couldn't just make the kingdom of Ridgedale bow down to him, he needed to crush it first. For a while he thought about creating a plague that would wipe out the men there, but after long thought he realized he needed some to survive, if he wanted to rule the rocks nothing more he could stay in Pullus.

The Dark Wizard cast his mind back many years ago to a time before Ridgedale was even founded. It was his father's fault he was the way he was, he was born to rule it was his birth right and his father took that from him. His father was Luca the First, at that time king of Easter dale the largest and wealthiest of the known lands. Raham as he was known then was the crown prince and set to inherit it the throne, even as a young man he couldn't wait. Then his father ruined his dreams and his life. He divorced his mother and wed the daughter of Gwilym monarch of Greenridge, thus he united the two kingdoms and Ridgedale was born. Raham and his mother and younger brother were expelled, banished, swept aside, forgotten, but Raham would not be silenced. Not long later his sibling and mother went missing, he never saw them again. He knew what happened to them though the king had them removed and so he fled. History recorded Luca as a great man, the father of a nation but Pravus knew better. Some years later he returned from his exile the crown was in dispute and Raham saw an opportunity, he had the support of a few older noblemen and a mercenary army. He was unsuccessful though, captured and dragged through the streets he was locked in stocks in the capital for days mocked and humiliated. If the king had known then what Pravus was to become he would have had him hanged. But Pravus was grateful in an odd way; he used those memories as fuel. He took his new name there in those stocks while people pointed and laughed at him. No one knew he had spent his exile studying sorcery and other dark arts, and when he was moved to a cell he used his skills to escape. His father had founded the kingdom, his father had sealed its fate.

He turned back and stepped into one of his many chambers. Like all his rooms it was mostly bare save for a large black cauldron bubbling away in the middle of this particular one. It stood over a small fire that offered most of the light in the room. He leaned over it muttering some incantations under his breath and waving his hands above it slightly.

The Dark Wizard knew much and he would find out exactly would it was that weighed on his mind. He had committed too much, worked too long for something unexpected to happen. He gripped the black hilt of his sword drew it and plunged it into the cauldron while he cast a spell. Smoke hissed and filled the room which seemed to shrink. When he withdrew the blade three dark masses sat on the steel, slowly these started to change form and within seconds had taken the form of ravens. Looking at the bird nearest the hilt Pravus ordered,

'Fly to Aurum, and report back what you see.' To the bird in the middle of the sword he said. 'Search the tower in Argentum I want to know what its captain has been up to recently.' To the last bird he simply commanded 'find

Marauder, quickly.' The Dark Wizard hadn't heard from his best spy since before the siege of Argentum started. With that the trio of dark ravens flew to the balcony and into the black night sky and almost immediately out of sight.

Leland wanted to pace round his chamber only his strength wouldn't allow it. He had summoned both his children to him an hour ago and still he waited. He had seen neither one for a few days now and that always concerned him, what were they up to? Every father worried about their sons, he thought, but he had more to worry about than most, not just their future but because it was linked to the kingdoms as well. He had built a magnificent capital here. It was a fine city before he took power but it was better now in every way. The architecture, the teachings, the economy the standard of life was so much greater in no small part thanks to him. And he had established a worthy counsel which oversaw his duties these past years.

He buried his head in his wrinkled hands as he thought that his one regret was that the light he shone on Aurum had not spread across the rest of the kingdom. According to reports more and more of the land was becoming lawless many of the outlying regions no longer recognised him as king. He knew he should not have ignored this but he had, instead he threw himself at making Civitas Aurum even greater. A shining example to follow. It was almost a city state. Argentum and the larger cities still followed his banner but Leland knew that the Lord and Knights of those cities held the real power. Men like Arian the Lord of the Silver tower and arguably the second most influential man in Ridgedale. The old king lifted his head and looked out of his chamber window. His grey eyes reflecting the weather outside perfectly. Not for the first time in his long life did he realise he had made a mistake with Arian. He had been happy to keep him at arm's length away out of sight from the paradise he had built here. Arian was a capable man like his fathers before him by letting him rule Argentum unchecked he had grown strong in more ways had first perceived. Not only had he an army that held back the might of Pullus for many years but he also had the love and support of the citizens there for doing so. But he wanted Arian to be strong, he needed it; a strong city in the west meant security in the east.

Leland cast his mind back to all those decades ago when he became king. He didn't inherit the throne he took it to save Ridgedale and his city. He was born to a noble family and had a seat on the ruling council at a young age, so it was he saw first-hand King Kraig IV's brutal regime. With such an unpopular monarch Leland was able to gain support to successfully oppose him. Kraig was banished, he made an ill-fated attempt to wrest the crown back but died doing so; the army fully backed Leland and were glad to see the tyrant deposed. Kraig's son made a lot of noise about rebelling against Leland but never did, his Grandson Kaine was it? He had the audacity to try some fifteen or twenty years ago but was quickly defeated in what was Lachlan's first taste of battle.

The king now thought of his wife who had died twenty five years ago at the ripe old age of 70. He missed her so, but she wasn't strong enough fight the fever she caught. Never short of an opinion and born in Argentum but even so he fell for her, what would she think of the state of the Silver City now.

He beat his arms down on his chair, and then rubbed his wrists at the pain he caused himself. When would his blasted sons arrive? They needed to know first that now things had turned sour for all. Word had just arrived that Argentum was being evacuated and the city was making a final stand. The king of Ridgedale like his citizens in the silver city had always believed Arian would never fail, he wouldn't allow the thought of it, and the results would not be pleasant. With hindsight, and he had plenty of it, he perhaps could have sent more support. Now it seemed he had to finally face the fact that his kingdom was at war. And at his age it was unlikely to see it out.

Recently this news caused him for the first time in his long life to feel old. He had started to look it more and more these past few years. Now he worried about his sons, he had always known they would present problems to his vision of the future and the way he saw it. Lachlan would plunder all the kingdoms coffers on war with Pullus, and Leuan he just schemed and plotted and that developed mistrust, not ideal when you rule. You need the people united behind you and bought into your vision. And Leland had that here, shame about the rest of Ridgedale he thought.

For the next two days Hcur and Chajak led the way as fast as they could through the old forest. They left the beaten track and followed old paths seldom used now. Bracken weeds and mosses covered what was left of the trail. Stopping only to rest and feed briefly they made good time. They spoke little, Chajak insisting they remained as silent as possible. To Austin it seemed like forever since they had seen anything but trees and bush, barely an animal or bird was to be seen. At one point the wood was made up of dense willow trees which seemed to hang low over them, Austin thought they would try and strangle him if they could. Late on the seventh night in the forest they set up camp near a quick moving stream which they had made the horses wade up for some distance hoping to lose their pursuit. Jak showed them her lightening reflexes by catching some fish barehanded which they cooked for supper over a small fire.

'Have we lost whoever following us?' Austin asked quietly while they ate. He hadn't asked for a while.

'The winds keep shifting, but I'm certain he's getting closer maybe only a few hours behind now.

'He?' asked the boy.

'For sure it's only one, probably male definitely one of your race.'

'And he seems to know his way around here like few other men do,' added Hcur, 'we've moved well now heading southeast towards the coast, there are no dwellings of men in the vicinity, yet our pursuer seems to know where were heading.'

'What, how?' gasped Austin.

'I've made an error,' Jak lowered her head. 'We make for the Fyord Bridge to cross over the river sovereign, trying to lose our hunter I decided, against Hcur's advice, to take this path in order to shake him of our trial and lose him in the wood. The plan hasn't succeeded and it seems now he will get their ahead of us...'

'So we will have to cross the sovereign elsewhere,' finished Hcur.

'You're certain he's headed there?' asked Austin.

'We are in the wilderness here, boy, I hoped he would follow us and ultimately get lost in the trees, but he has read our intent and I'm certain he is now making a direct path to the bridge.'

'But are we certain of his intentions? He asked 'If he's followed us this far he might be from Argentum, maybe he brings news for us? Or perhaps he's a refugee from the city taking his chances away from the main caravan heading to Aurum just like ourselves.'

'That might be true enough, young one,' Hcur piped in, 'but he has followed us skilfully for two days now and my instincts cry out trouble. It is not out of the question that he knows of the sword and is headed here to take it from you. That is what we believe and why we will steer clear of him. I do not like nor do I trust strangers in the woods.'

'But father said no one else knows of the sword, he ...'

'No one that we know of, my lad, but the enemy has many spies,' Hcur interrupted.

'And while we trust your father, we don't trust where his information may sometimes come from. Men can be deceitful willingly or not,' added Jak. 'We will camp here and get up at first light, the river is close now we will find a way to get over somehow before we get the Fyord Bridge, and then we carry on east hoping our shadow loses our trial.' With that Chajak pulled out her blanket and lit her small candle and she made herself comfy on the ground.

'I'll take first watch then!' laughed Hcur at his friend's actions.

The hard forest floor was just about okay for sitting and eating Austin thought but all the small stones and twigs wouldn't be great for sleeping on.

'Will there be somewhere better to camp further on?' he asked and Hcur let out a chuckle as he unpacked his own blanket.

'Maybe further on the floor is even worse, at least it's still warm here.' As he settled down Austin asked the cat a question.

'What is that candle for Jak? you light it every night?'

'It is a sacred candle, our culture believe it wards evil spirits away. Traditionally we make candles if we are planning a journey, that way even when I'm away from home the spirits know a fire still burns in my heart and my instincts are still sharp.' There was a long pause and all could see the dejection in the cat's eyes, her instincts had led them to take this route.

'Tell me about that rope?' Hcur changed the subject. 'Your father said it saved his life?'

'Well the story starts years ago when Dad led the guard for the first time against the dark army. Sinister had taken a foothold on the Evermoor fields and father was determined to force them back. He said it was pitch black and the enemy had gone quiet and he and a few scouts had ventured to find out why. They made for a ditch they could see as dad reckoned it would provide some cover.' Austin pulled the rope from his bag. 'Anyway right before they get in it he trips over this and lands face down just as a hail of arrows fly low over their position and fatally pierced the armour of his two companions. It hurt him deeply that they would never return home with him. He told me that the rope stood a roughly three inches from the ground tied to metal pegs. He heard a commotion around him and looked up to see the army of Pullus was making a charge. He grabbed the rope to pull himself up quickly but it gave way, it wasn't secure to the pegs.

'So how had it tripped him?' Jak asked.

'Father didn't have the time to find out, he grabbed it and ran back to his defences. He never knew who put it there or for what reason but he kept it close ever since. He always considered it lucky.' He tossed the rope gently to Chajak who looked at it closely. It didn't look remarkable, though it looked almost silvery in the dark light.

'Father says it's about 15 feet long, but it'll double the length it seems.'

'What, how?' Jak scoffed still looking at the rope.

'I don't know but I believe him,' put in Hcur. 'Also I think we have a new way of crossing the river.' He winked at Austin.

Marauder had almost lost his quarry in the deep forest more than once. When he made the decision to pursue them he had to go return to his tired horse and then pick up their trail from where they entered to forest. It had not been easy; he had given them a big head start and had travelled cautiously, whoever he was following knew how to protect their tracks. In the dark of night Marauder was almost invisible in his dark green robes. His keen eyes peered out of his hood lost in thought. He was hidden from view from all but the sharpest of eyes. For a week now he had followed them but soon he'll have his prey. Silently he rested high up on the last strong branch in a rotten tree. The group he chased had left Argentum in a hurry and not with the mass currently and slowly making for Aurum. They were headed through the wild and using terrain seldom used by anyone. To what end? He mused. Several times he had thought about breaking off his pursuit after all he was only following them because of the intrigue. Maybe they had something important, they could be carrying any number of documents or artefacts deemed valuable enough to smuggle out of the city.

He was quite unlike his cousin. Marauder was cool calculating and very patient, not hot tempered and impetuous like Malice. He had no other purpose in life, brought up a nomad always roaming the lands with his uncle and cousin. He had never known his grandfather the king. He had heard many mention him as a tyrant, he believed them. He knew Malice and his father could be cruel men and he didn't doubt King Kraig was also. But his fate was to follow cousin and now to work for Pravus, another bitter and evil man. But he was paid very well, and if he the Sorcerer delivered half his promises Marauder knew he would be an extremely wealthy man for the rest of his life. That didn't mean his would ever trust him though. A wise man learns more from his enemies than a fool learns from his friends, Marauder was no fool and he had no friends.

He was sure that they now knew he was following them, they had picked up there pace considerably two days ago. And no one would venture the paths they had taken unless trying to lose someone. They now seemed to be headed in the direction of Tombstone or one of any number of small towns east of the River Sovereign. He had decided to head them off at the Fyord Bridge the only crossing in these parts and even though they were three they would need to be very skilled to stand against him that is if they even saw him here.

But they weren't here yet. Judging by their pace they should have been by now unless they had stopped completely. And they wouldn't do that there was no reason to spend so long out there in the bush. Unless they had read his intent. They hadn't underestimated him but he had them. He cursed aloud as he looked across to the bridge. That could only mean they knew a way to cross someplace else. Marauder almost threw himself out of the tree and sprinted back to his horse. He didn't see a raven high above him in the trees spring from branch to branch before following him.

'So you want us to cross here?' asked Austin incredulously. They stood next to a ravine the river flowed powerfully over sharp rocks some twenty feet down, the other side was about the same distance away. 'How are we going to manage that?'

Chajak looked across before speaking, the white rock walls shone in the morning sun.

'I'll leap across taking one end of Austin's rope with me the other end will be tied here then you will shimmy across to the other side.'

'Agreed.' Hcur pointed at some tree roots sticking out near the edge. 'We can tie the cord here.'

'That's a big drop into some dangerous moving water guys. Isn't there somewhere better?'

'Ha you always think there's somewhere better, young Austin. Sometimes there is but often there is not,' spoke the wise bird. He took the rope from Austin and tied it to a sturdy root of a tree near the edge. He held the other end by his chest and nodded at the Cat while walking closer to the ravine.

Chajak walked to the cover of the forest and looked back to the river. She couldn't see the water just the drop which it was at the bottom of and the noise it made as it washed over the rocks. She crouched down and took a deep breath. Both feet planted together she then raced forward with incredible acceleration. Austin could only look on he knew it was the plan but hadn't expected it so suddenly though. Just as Jak reached the edge Hcur guided the rope into her reach. The cheetah grabbed it cleanly and leapt across the Sovereign in one motion. She landed hard against the opposite side her chest hitting the solid rock while her hands pawed for grip to keep her up. Quick as a flash she took a knife from her belt and buried it in the earth using the handle as a lever to climb up.

The rope made the distance with some to spare. Chajak surveyed her side and seeing nothing close to tie it to she pulled out her swords and drove them into the dirt with all her strength. Decorative claws on the end of her swords seemed to reach out from the ground to the sky. She then put her feet against them and took the strain of the rope and urged her companions across.

'One at a time please,' she laughed.

'Good job, my friend,' shouted Hcur over to her. 'So who's first?' Austin knew this wasn't a real question Hcur wouldn't leave him on this side alone. But he was stunned by Chajak's achievement and still coming to terms with the drop below.

'If we fall we'll be swept away for certain,' he said.

'If the rocks don't get you first!' Jak scoffed.

'Don't fall then.' Hcur gave a beaky grin. 'You're up.'

'We haven't got all day now!' shouted Chajak. Austin edged up to the side of the ravine and crouched down and took the line.

'What's the best way to cross Hcur?'

'Grab hold tight wrap your feet after you and shimmy over.'

'So don't dangle?' Austin replied again.

'No, let your legs do some work, too, it'll be easier.'

Austin reached for the rope but when he looked at Hcur kneeling next to him he knew the bird could see the fear in his eyes.'

'If I could carry you across I would, can you manage, young one?' he asked earnestly.

'I don't know, but I'll try,' was his reply.

'That's all I can ask for.' Hcur took a wrap of fabric from around his waist and tied it around Austin's wrists which still held the rope. 'That should hold you if your grip should fail, a word of advice remember in everything we do our own thoughts can help us succeed or they can cause us to fail. Always maintain a positive attitude.'

'Okay here goes.' And with that Austin started to cross. He took a few minutes taking care each time he moved his hands over the rope. He didn't look down, not once, he dared himself not too. Sometimes the rope swayed sideways a little in the wind but Austin didn't let it stop him at first.

Hcur remained silent still kneeling on the bank willing the boy across when at just over halfway Austin stopped and screamed out.

'It's too far I can't do it.' His hands ached from holding the rope so tight.

'You can,' shouted Jak, 'believe that you can we know you can.'

'My hands hurt.' he yelled out again. 'It's too far.'

'It'll hurt more if you fall,' Jak snapped.

'You're close no matter how far you think you are away, and every inch gets you closer,' shouted Hcur. Slowly Austin got going again when he neared the far side Jak lunged at him and hauled him up.

'I made it.' It was a few moments before he released his grip on his companion. Chajak gave him a smile and a hug before resuming her position.

He looked at his hands they were bright red from his tight grip on the line and adrenaline still raced through his body.

'Well done, boy. Are you ready, my old friend?' she shouted across the river.

'The question is are you ready for me' Hcur replied. He took his mace and his shield from over his shoulders and hurled them both to the over side of the sovereign along with a small satchel he carried.

Hcur then started to cross the river, when he left the bank Chajak was pulled forward some but held her grip visibly straining. The bird was bigger than them all. Austin went to her side and tried to take as big a load off as he could. The Hawk was making good progress when a figure in the distance caught Jak's attention.

'We have company.'

'Hcur looked back but could see nothing from his vantage point.' Suddenly a small dart whistled through the air and pierced his right boot. The hawk let out a yell and his legs fell from the rope but his feathered fingers held tight.

'Austin grab the shield and cover us,' growled Chajak. He did as ordered and not before time. A few more quarrels bounced off it as the figure in the distance took aim at them. 'Can you make it?' the cat called to Hcur.

'Any advice you may have for me make it brief,' came the answer.

'He's not aiming now instead he's running toward us, get here fast.' Hcur pulled himself to the side of the ravine with all his might ignoring the pain in his ankle.

'He's firing again!' yelled Austin. Both he and Jak scrambled forward to protect their friend once he was on the edge no longer needing the rope. Another dart hit Hcur in the shoulder this time but they managed to pull him up. Chajak then yanked Austin's bow from his shoulders pulling him over in the process and fired a volley of arrows as quick as she could manage. The shots were wild but close enough to make the attacker dive for cover.

'Take shelter in the trees behind me, take him with you.' They didn't need telling twice they turned and ran. Austin didn't know why but he reached for the rope as he turned. It came freely with him as if it wasn't even tied across the other side of the Sovereign. Once in the safety of the cover provided by the trees they turned back to see what where Jak was. Moments later she sprinted towards them followed by a hail of quarrels that imbedded deep into the trees, her two swords in one hand and the bow the other, she returned it to Austin and she grabbed Hcur. 'Let's keep moving shall we. Who knows how long it'll take our assailant to cross the bank.' As they turned and carried on east, a raven took flight across the bank and swiftly headed west.

Chapter V: Dark Times

They had come at last. Lachlan and Leuan arrived together at the great door to the throne room finally answering their father's summons.

'Little brother I see you've been drawn away from all you're scheming to finally visit father. I'm surprised you remember where he is it's been that long, or was that the problem, you got lost on your way?' mocked the Colossus. Leuan just sneered.

'So what's your excuse for being late? Busy playing soldiers again?'

'I've been with my men yes,' was the reply, 'war is coming to Ridgedale I feel it, time for little cowards to run and hide while men become heroes.'

'Funny that isn't it, you can make plans but all I do is scheme. Are they not one and the same? You might not see it because of all your bravado but I care deeply about this kingdom, too.' With that Leuan pushed open the chamber door and stepped inside. Lachlan followed closely slamming the doors behind him. The council all looked on from the large table as they marched towards their father with the exception of Silos at the head of them, his gaze remained intently on the papers in front of him.

'Where in the name of all that is good have you two been?' spat out the king. It wasn't very often he got angry. He looked over his councillors. 'Leave us now,' he demanded. The Conniving looked straight ahead as they quickly left refusing to meet the desperate eyes of Silos who now looked over. When the door was once again closed silence filled the throne room. Light poured in through the high massive windows on three of its sides, the sons stood meters apart in front of their father.

'Well can't my sons speak?'

'Forgive my delay, Father, I have been engaged, together with the guard, putting our heads together knocking about some ideas,' boomed Lachlan.

'That's explains the smell of stale ale,' spoke Leuan quietly. If Leland heard the comment he let it go.

'When your king summons you, you drop what you are doing. When your father summons you likewise.' He raged. Both his sons' heads dropped.

'I'm sorry father,' they said in unison. The old king paused and calmed himself.

'I have ill news from Argentum I'm afraid.' Lachlan took a step forward, Leuan's eyes narrowed. 'A pigeon arrived yesterday morning with a message. The city is all but lost,' he said solemnly. 'It has probably fallen in the time is has taken you to arrive.'

'I knew it would be so,' shouted the eldest 'for how long have I said we need to march out to the silver city?'

'Now is not the time for I-told-you-so's son now we need to help the refuges marching here.'

'What news of Arian?' said Leuan almost a whisper. Leland held a small parchment up.

'It's from one of his lieutenants, it says the Dark Lord Pravus has unleashed his biggest assault yet and the city can no longer hold off the evil forces. We can only speculate what has now happened.'

'What will we do now?' said Lachlan.

'I have already sent out our quickest scouts to meet the citizens fleeing Argentum. Some will ride on to try and gather more information from the silver city. But I already fear the worst.' He bowed his head.

'Send me out my king. My guards are the best let The Black Sorcerer taste the steel of our swords.'

'I agree with my brother, my king, he is a formidable warrior the enemies of our kingdom would be hard pressed to oppose him.' Both turned to look at Leuan. Lachlan did not speak but wondered what the wheels turning in his brother's mind were up to, Leuan had never agreed with him before. If Lachlan said the sky was blue Leuan would agree to his last breath it was red.

'We feel differently the council and me. What you will do is go to the mountain fortifications Lachlan and bolster our troops there.'

'But...' the Colossus tried to interject. Leland held up his hand to stop him.

'You will also send word to Krul's folly and Civitas Aeris and all our other garrisons around the kingdom to send men to join you at the Ridgegate. If and it's a big if at the present, Pravus marches east we'll meet him in the mountains. We need to be prepared for the worst until we know what the evil one's plans are.' They all knew that would take time though; the Sapphire Sea far to the south of them separated Aeris, the bronze castle, from the rest of the nation. Other garrisons weren't much closer, it would be days before some got the message.

'We could use the chargers now,' Lachlan said almost to himself. The men of Aeris in the cold lands of Praeter were known as the chargers and considered fearless since they took the aggressive woolly Rhino as their crest centuries ago.

'How will we break this to the populace, Father? You've hid news of Sinister from them for so long,' asked Leuan.

'No good will come from spreading the news, panic won't help us.'

'Forgive me, Father, but hasn't the truth been kept from them for long enough, continuing this lie…'

'Kings do not lie!' Leland beat his hands down against the arms of his throne. 'But neither do I have to indulge all facts to the masses.' Leuan gave a small bow.

'You are wise and have ruled for so long I have no doubt you know what's best my king I just want to explore every…'

'Forget the masses,' interrupted Lachlan, 'we do have to worry about Sinister we have to worry about the army marching from Pullus. Why don't you see that waiting for him to strike at us will result in the same fate as Argentum. We need to lash out first!

'Any force would do well to break past our defences in the mountains, my son. Especially with you leading them. I've always been reluctant to let you too far from my sight, the both of you, be glad I'm giving you this chance, this opportunity to be saviour of our kingdom. You would march to meet him now unprepared? That would be folly and it would be your demise.' Leland looked at his first born sternly. He needed to say no more Lachlan would do as ordered. He gestured and the Colossus took his usual seat by his king's side.

'What would my king ask of me in this unfortunate time?' asked Leuan, his arms open.

'Do you desire to take up arms and aid your brother?'

'Not really a task I'm best suited for,' The Conniving squirmed.

'I thought as much, tell me what you are...' the king stopped himself. Leuan's eyes narrowed once again. 'I've need for you on the council, my son. Some of my elder councillors distrust Silos though they are rather vague as to why. I want you to get to the bottom of this the council must be united now more than ever.'

'Very well, my King I well see to the matter at once.'

'For the first time in as long as I can remember, my boys, things are happening that are out of my control.' The sons shared concerned glances at each other. 'I pray now that were not too late to react but I fear it is so.'

The last raven had at last returned to Pravus. The first confirmed what he already knew, that Argentum had fallen and that Malice was fortifying the city and reorganizing the Goblyn hordes waiting for word to march on. The second raven had only revealed that the King of Ridgedale was aware of the trouble the sorcerer was creating but had done little about it as yet. Pravus had expected as much he had other spies in Aurum that also confirmed this. But what of Marauder what was he up to? The Dark Prince held his sword to the raven now perched on the window. It hopped on to the blade and Pravus carried it to the cauldron then plunged it back into the mix from which it had come. When the sword was withdrawn images began to appear in the bubbling liquid, first of Marauder's journey through the forest, then his quick sprint to the bridge. Where is he going thought the sorcerer? Then from the bird's vantage point high in the trees the images showed his lieutenant firing at strangers crossing a river. A boy and two others. It been many years since Pravus had dealt with their kind; he sneered, filthy animals, he had thought the great cat and birds were now extinct. The images slowly bubbled away. Marauder had been right to follow them now he had to find out what they were doing. Why had they now raised their flea bitten heads from whatever hovel they had hidden in he mused. He didn't like the timing. Once more his evil sword entered the foul liquid more spells were muttered only this time the black mass formed a large bat.

'Learn all you can about the boy and his animal companions,' he hissed and the bat flew on obeying its master.

Austin and Jak were worried about Hcur, his heavy boots had taken most of the impact of one quarrel but the other in his shoulder had cut deep and bled considerably. They sat by some trees the Cat being satisfied they had put enough distance between them and their attacker for now. The night was drawing in.

'He'll be okay won't he, Jak?' asked Austin.

'If we can treat him he should be. I've stopped the bleeding for now, but we need shelter for the night. It is going to rain I can feel it. Hcur sat up against a tree.

'I agree rain is on its way.'

'Then where do we go?' Austin wanted to know.

'Tombstone isn't far north up the river this side. It's not where we intended to go but it'll have to do, Hcur you need a good rest and I need better light to check your wounds.' The bird seemed to ponder this then reluctantly agreed.

'Who was it that attacked us?' said Austin after a few moments. Jak examined one of the darts removed from his friend. It was small, about three inches long. Like a tiny solid arrow, extremely sharp was its tip.

'I have never encountered a weapon like this, lad.' She pocketed it, looking all around as if she expected to be ambushed once more. 'But for certain right now we will spend all our energy on getting our friend here to safety.' Looking at Austin she continued, 'Help me carry him and we will speculate more later.'

They pushed on the ground started to rise and fall with slopes some quite steep, the trees gave way to heathers and the and as expected the skies soon opened.

'Tell me everything you know, Silos, all that council has learned of events in the west?' Leuan spoke in his quite tone. They were in a small room off the great hall; a few hours had passed since the council was dismissed. They both stood by the window looking down on the courtyard. They watched as Lachlan and his troops made ready to leave for the mountains. The Colossus had wasted little time eager for battle he hoped would come his way.

'My Prince, our intelligence has suspected for some time this strike on Civitas Argentum was coming, indeed it was also felt the city was on a knife-edge.

'And still the Constant did nothing?'

'You know your father, he buried his head in the sand about such matters, until this news he had barely addressed the councillors about the city in months.

'Anything else I should know?'

'There was another message from the Silver City a few hours prior to our learning of the city's impending doom. Though it has not reached the council's ears ...' Out in the yard Lachlan finished barking his orders to his men. He lifted his huge broadsword into the air, its blade was wide and it had a diamond shaped hole in it close to the hilt and its golden handle, a lad could put his hand through that gap. His normal golden armour now boasted a gold helmet and great shield, he signalled forward and led his forces away on horseback. The cheering that accompanied them could be heard far and wide. When Lachlan had all but disappeared from view Leuan turned to Silos. He raised his eyebrow.

'And what was this news most unworthy of the council then?'

'I have a source in Argentum that I trust though the council don't know of him. It is believed though not confirmed that Arian had sent his son from harm's way it also implies Arian had given the boy a package of some sort.'

'Do we know what?'

'My source says he tied it to his son's horse, we don't know what it is though.' 'This is news? It's not unusual for a Father to want his children out of harm's way.' The wheels in Leuan's head were already turning many possible reasons. His gut told him this was important, he looked back to the window. 'The parcel could be anything, a family heirloom, and provisions for the road perhaps.'

'The child of Arian left with two companions,' continued Silos as he took a seat next to a small table and poured himself some wine from a bottle sat there. 'My source doesn't know who they were. He is certain they are not part of the city guard and didn't recognise them as prominent citizens of Argentum either. But they were hooded.'

'Tell me more about your source.'

'I have many sources planted around the kingdom, my Prince, the regional Lords and Captains often omit many important details in their reports to the king for various self-serving reasons.' He made a dismissive gesture with his hand, 'My agents help me provide a fuller picture of life in Ridgedale, I've personally selected them all and none are more vital than my agent in the Silver City.

Leuan gave a little laugh over his shoulder before looking out the window once more. 'And people call me conniving! I knew there was a reason we sought each other out councillor. We think very much alike. If it concerns the smooth running of the kingdom a leaf will not fall from a tree that you do not know about it seems. What is the destination of the trio?'

'We know not, they left in dead of night and in almost total secrecy.'

'That information may prove important, council leader, I suggest you alert some other of your sources to keep their eyes more alert than usual.' Silos nodded in agreement he hadn't taken his eyes off the Prince. 'In the meantime should my father ask I've been trying to broker peace in the council some members don't seem don't trust you I can't think why.'

With that Leuan made to leave the room but stopped at the door then through the council leader the briefest of glances. 'Keep me informed.'

The convoy looked large even from this height. Venom could see hundreds of people tread a path westwards. From her vantage point far above them the dragon thought that the caravan of horses, carts and folk almost looked like a giant snake slithering away. She hated snakes, her large dark eyes flashed with anger at the thought of them. Her dark silhouette was now in contrast to the midday sun around her. She was long of tail and had a short thick neck, a massive wingspan and two dozen or so triangular plates ran down her spine like shark's teeth to her tail in staggered pairs. She also had three massive horns both on her tail and her head where two sat on her brow the other above her nose. The folk below were mostly unarmed. Fleeing from their homes to the safe haven of the capital. Or so they thought. She had let them march for a few days now, so they would build up their hopes free from immediate danger, in a day they would reach the mountains, but they would be tired from their journey – Easy targets – they didn't even know she was stalking them. She flashed her many razor-sharp white teeth.

Dozens had already left the procession below, seeking sanctuary in other towns and villages rather than be led all the way through the mountains to Aurum. Several of these she had already feasted on. She knew, though, many of them had to survive the trek they were on, so then they could spread the fear to the rest of the land. Fear was a powerful weapon.

Venom knew of no others like her, all the dragons had been killed centuries ago in Ridgedale. She gave up searching elsewhere for others a long time ago. When she was summoned to Acerbus by Pravus's spell she was livid at first, unable to comprehend what he had done to her, but she soon realised his power and accepted his request to join him.

She had her limitations she knew that, but between them they would rule these lands like a dragon should.

She paused hovering for a moment her giant wings slowly flapping in the air. A hint of a smile cracked across her black features and showed her huge teeth. Then with a thunderous roar and a giant eruption of flame that lit up the sky, she announced her presence to those below. They tried to escape but it was too late.

Leuan almost seemed to glide back to his personal quarters, his arms always crossed when he walked, hands hidden in his flowing sleeves. Back in his sanctuary in a far wing of the tower he began to think of his brother. Watching him leave for the mountains he felt nothing but now he realised his brother had actually gone. Would he ever return to see their father again? The conniving now knew his fate was in the hands of the country's enemy. He needed the Evil Wizard's forces to slay his brother then he would be next in line.

The only doubt he now had was about Pravus himself, just how strong were his Dark Forces and would he be able to come an agreement with him?

That if it was a him. Old tales say he was a ghost a spectre something to fear behind his terrible power. Leuan never believed this, Pravus was just a man, just exceptionally long lived even more so than his father. Other tales said he was even Luca's son. Leuan knew his sorcery must be strong to have lived for so long but he was mortal. Flesh and bone. And like all men he must have a weakness. He had spent many hours trying to find it and he wouldn't rest until he did. His future depended on it.

Chapter VI: The Criminal

Braydon was a criminal. He was now locked in a cage paying for his crime. Once he had served as an archer in the Royal army of Ridgedale. Usually he would back up his fellow troops no matter what scrapes they would get into and he was known to get into some scrapes also. They all had each other's backs and all that, and soldiers can get rowdy when off duty can't they? His captain was a large, round, obnoxious man, red of face with untidy ginger hair and whiskers. A few days back the captain had gotten very drunk in Tombstone, he had attacked a young barmaid. Braydon now felt he couldn't continue to turn a blind eye. A line needed to be drawn. He planted his superior with a punch so hard it took him off his chubby feet and clear over the bar. So now Braydon was a criminal.

And here he was hanging in a cage not tall enough to stand in, that swung from a mighty branch of a strong old tree. On another branch two pieces of long and worn rope hung and swayed in the light breeze. He sat legs dangling out slowly swinging. Two other cages swung either side of him. A vile little man who cursed a lot and stank so much it made Braydon gag was to his left. The other cage to his right was bottomless and therefore empty. Tied nearby to a grey tree with twisted leafless branches were two skeletons, yet more nooses hung from its branches, and twenty yards ahead of him was a very old rotten-looking gallows. Nothing else was nearby except for more of those nasty looking trees and the path to Tombstone which could be seen off in the distance.

Syzmon the vile occupant of the other cage snored coarsely, the quietest he had been for hours. Braydon had dark skin and gentle brown eyes, his usual bald head now had a little patchy growth and his usual neat black beard was starting to become unkempt. He wore rags, his uniform long since stripped away. There was no water in his cell and no one had passed since he had been left there two days ago. He had given up trying to escape the cage; the bars and the lock wouldn't budge. It seemed all he and his neighbour had to look forward to was a slow death. A few droplets of rain started to fall.

The city had fallen, Malice thought it would be easier but it had been taken at last. The last survivors had been routed from their hiding places, the Captain of the guard and Lord of the Tower had fallen to his very hand. He had put up a brave fight, but he was no match in the end. Malice stood in the courtyard near the tower doors taking in the scene, a few fires still smouldered. The once great white walls of the castle were now almost black down here at its base. A Goblyn lieutenant approached him.

'The last captive is disposed of, sir,' it hissed.

Malice just shook his head; he had ordered all prisoners killed, he didn't want to waste effort guarding or bothering to feed them. Most troops of the city had fought to the death and the few that were caught were no longer an issue.

'And the sword?' he asked the Goblyn. They glanced over to a spot in the wall where several more Goblyns looked busy. There in the wall was a sword buried about shoulder height deep in the stone almost to its hilt. The troops were furiously trying to free it. Many had torn shreds off their hands trying. It was the tower captain's sword the mighty Arian, and he wanted it. Spoils of war. The Wyrm, as the weapon was known to the dark troops, was known to have slain many of their kind.

'It remains set, we can't release it.'

'Pathetic slime, get out of my sight.' Malice struck the lieutenant hard in the face with the back of hand. When the lieutenant had fled he strode powerfully towards the tower but something stopped him short of the door, a puddle near it had started bubbling away, then a great cloud of steam erupted from it. The cloud turned black which slowly evaporated to reveal the shadow of the Dark Lord himself.

Making himself appear in Argentum was no easy spell even for a wizard with his skill. He took in everything around him, the courtyard the fires the smells, while he regained his composure. Malice was in front of him on one knee head bowed Pravus made no motion for him to get up.

So this is Argentum the dark wizard thought, he hadn't decided whether or not to level it yet, Civitas Acerbus would always be his capital other cities were unimportant. But back to the matter in hand.

'I've a mission for the Raptors,' he hissed at Malice.

The old town of Tombstone was once a prosperous port on the Sovereign and a stopover for miners digging for gold in the mountains. Formerly known as Wetstone the money brought by prospectors and miners had long gone, gold was no longer to be found in these parts. To make matters worse for the town all the digging up river had destroyed the landscape and sedimentary and rubble had drifted downstream and silted up the port. Ships could no longer sail close to the bank even if they still had reason to come. The long sandstone sea wall now looked out across marshland, a marooned wooden galleon in a sea of long grass a hint to the river that had all but abandoned the town. The powerful Sovereign was once wide here now it could just about be seen in the distance. In its heyday more money passed through here than in Civitas Aurum itself but the place had gone to rack and ruin since then and very few folk remained here now.

A few stores barely made enough to get by; the inn was the only place left that still thrived. Frequented by travellers and the locals alike *The Pen and the Sword* was always a lively place in stark contrast with the rest of the town. Even more so when the soldiers were around.

Austin and Chajak aided the Hcur on this stretch of the journey, his injuries worsened and meant he needed a good night's rest and some attention, Chajak could help heal him but not in the damp. They needed a room. None of them wanted to go to the town but what choice did they have?

They paused and took some shelter from the downpour in a dilapidated barn on the outskirts of the town.

'Is there nowhere better to stay are any of the buildings here abandoned?' asked Austin.

'It would take too long to find out boy, the inn is the best option we all need rest and shelter from the rain, and the food wouldn't go amiss either. Stick to the plan Austin and we will be fine,' answered Chajak. Soon they moved on towards the inn, Tombstone looked much like a ghost town on a busy day, but in the pouring rain on this night the place was particularly eerie. Wrapped up in their cloaks they trudged up the muddy streets with caution. When they reached the door Jak patted Austin on the shoulder then helped Hcur around to the side and out of sight, Austin nervously entered. He gripped the sword still wrapped tightly in the now soaking cloth. He held it low and under his cloak hoping to keep it out of sight. He had thought of giving it to his companions while he sorted the room but couldn't bear to part with it. He removed his hood and shook off the rain as he approached a large bar in the middle of the vast room. The inn was bigger than it looked on the outside. A few patrons sat on stools talking to the barkeeper and ten or so soldiers massed by a huge fireplace which was burning brightly, they barely looked up at him.

The barman dragged himself away from his friends and headed over to Austin.

'And how may I help a young guest on this damp night?' he was almost as broad as he was tall, thick shaggy brown hair and a similar beard; he wiped his hands across his dirty apron then put them on the bar.

'I need a room for the night, I've been caught out by the weather,' Austin answered. 'I'm on my way to Northridge Vale but my camp is sodden tonight. I've heard good things about the inn and thought it must be better than the rain.' He added.

'Indeed so, my guest, I'll have a room prepared hastily but first a drink?'

'Something warm please.' Austin nodded in agreement.

'Welcome then to *The Pen and the Sword*, the house of Gwilym with the finest hospitality your find in these parts,' With that he let out a laugh then made hot tea, Austin surveyed the bar more closely, the barman's friends looked him over regularly but they seemed harmless enough. The soldiers still barely noticed him, and for that he was grateful. A drink was set on the bar for him and he drank it quickly and ordered another. Gwil the barman returned and announced the room was ready.

'As an inn keep named after a king I offer my kingly hospitality, last on the left that way, enjoy.'

Austin gathered his bag and new drink and left the innkeeper some gold coins and quickly retired to it.

He shut the door locked it and headed straight to the window and opened it wide, the rain rushed in along with the cold. It seemed it was raining even harder now, he looked down into a narrow alley but couldn't see much in it through the darkness. He whistled and waited. After a few moments he could make out movement. Austin tied his rope to the sturdy looking bed and tossed the other end out of the window; almost immediately Jak climbed up the rope with Hcur across her shoulders. The cat bundled the hawk into the room then Austin helped him to the only bed then shut the window tight. They all rested for a moment, then took off their sodden cloaks and hung them by the fire that was roaring in the corner, along with everything else in their packs.

Jak did what she could for Hcur and was satisfied the wounds were healing well enough.

'And you can continue our journey with a limp, as I am no longer carrying you!' she jested. Soon all their sodden clothes were drying by the fire and they settled down. Austin had been sent for more food and drink, Gwilym must have wondered how one lad could put so much food away but if he did he kept it to himself. Jak had paid for it with a stack of gold coins she produced, Austin decided against asking where they came from for now, but he made a mental note to ask her later.

'Is now a good time to ask about the attack?' he asked instead.

'You can ask, but I know as much as you,' replied Jak. 'We were followed for quite some time, and evidently he realised we weren't going to cross at the bridge and upped his pursuit.'

'We need to be even more careful from now on,' added Hcur. 'We don't know our attacker or his motives, but we should assume this phantom pursuing us will try again.'

'Do you think he really knows of the sword?' Wondered Austin aloud. Jak and Hcur looked at each other, neither could answer.

'What if he's still following us?'

'We can't rule it out, lad, he has followed us far, but he would do well to pick up our trail so fast. None the less we continue early in the morning so perhaps we should get our heads down,' said Jak as she settled into a big chair in the corner.

'I'll take the floor then,' said Austin grabbing a blanket. As they all made themselves comfy, Hcur recited an old poem.

Forged stronger than the earth
Its return and our rebirth
True symbol from tip to hilt
Its legend shall never wilt
An eternity it will endure
The Guardian's blade forever more
A flock behind it we will gather
Its enemies will fear and scatter

'What's that?' asked Austin.

'We used to say that in the Aerie. Remember, lad, the Guardian's sword is not just important to your kind but to all of us,' said the hawk softly.

'What do you know about Pravus, Hcur? My father would never speak of him.'

'I know as much as any I suppose, that is to say I don't know very much. An old story would tell of him being a young and arrogant prince before he became the monster we know now.'

'Tell me about Skull Rock, lad' asked Jak. 'I know the cats were involved but I don't know much about it?'

'The cats were there?' Austin was puzzled.

'A battle long before both of you came along,' answered the Hawk. 'You may know the first battle of Skull Rock was a war lasting several years in which your armies laboured to rid the Goblyns from their foothold in that region.' Austin nodded in agreement. 'Well the second battle of Skull rock was a lot shorter than the first largely due to one reason. The great cats *were* involved. One hundred of them had travelled west on an expedition to learn more of the lands, and they were accompanied by Apollo the Eagle, they did this every generation. As was custom they avoided man, it was part of the exercise to avoid such large numbers being spotted and they always succeeded. Apollo was about to make his secret trip to the Silver Tower to send his greetings to its Guardian when the conflict broke out. Apollo could have turned around and returned to safety, he was after all to have nothing to do with man. But instead he convinced the cats to help fight the Goblyn masses. They circled around the Evermoor and attacked Skull Rock from its east side. The Goblyns didn't see it coming and were routed. The men who were facing defeat didn't see it coming either. The Lord of the silver tower, your great great grandfather it seems, Austin, went personally to thank these strangers and while doing so saved Apollo from a stray Goblyn raid.'

'What did he do?' asked Jak.

'I've asked Apollo many times he would not tell me,' replied the hawk honestly. 'But it is one reason as to why he never abandoned dialogues between our races and men and why his son won't either. One thing we do know is that men with a very few exceptions aren't aware that they owe the cats a great deal.'

'That must be why Apollo gave Abel these gauntlets' Austin looked at the Silver on his wrists. 'He saved his life.'

'So it seems, a very generous gift indeed. A small debt, though, compared to a life.'

'Weren't dragons involved in the war, too?' asked Austin.

'Dragons no, just one a huge beast. It almost won Pravus the war. But I'll speak no more of dragons tonight.' With that he closed his eyes and drifted off.

They set off early the next day all the much happier for some sheltered rest for the first time in days. And although he would never admit it Hcur appreciated the comfy mattress, too. His wound was strapped up and if it bothered him he showed no sign of it that Austin could see. Leaving Tombstone they left the Sovereign behind also and it now veered off westerly towards the mountains and its icy spring. They headed north up a drenched muddy path. The rain had gone and the day was cool but not too cold, all they had to worry about for the moment was the mud. As they slugged through it leaving the town behind the track became almost bog like. Far off in the distance was the great mountain range. The original plan was for them to cross the mountains there then it was a trek northeast to Aurum. But now they would continue east again and across the southern plains. They trudged now slowly towards some greyish trees up ahead, one was a giant grey oak but others nearby Austin didn't recognise. None of these trees had any leaves just many twisting thin branches, they weren't particularly tall but they looked menacing none the less. He imagined they might try and grab him if they walked too close.

'What's in that big tree ahead?' he asked as they got closer.

'Its three traps, young one. We shouldn't get to close, Hcur, it's the gallows tree.' The bird nodded his agreement and although his hood was up he tried pulling it further.

'This is a forsaken place, Austin. I had forgotten we would pass it. Many men have lost their lives here. Do not go near the trees for their bark is poisonous and will kill you should feel its touch for too long.' This was the only place in Ridgedale these trees lived now, the rest having been burnt or chopped down. While many trees, plants and herbs had leaves and fruits that can heal it was the opposite with these trees. Its bark was deadly to touch for too long and it's tempting looking purple berries even more perilous Hcur explained, 'It has even been known for men to smear arrow heads in there toxic amber making them twice as deadly.'

'Your people tie criminals to these trees as punishment for capital crimes,' sneered Jak. 'An eye for an eye one would guess...' she shook her head slowly.' But it's a slow way to die.'

'That's barbaric,' gasped Austin. 'And against the law surely?' He had heard of the tree of death but thought it a myth just like birds and cats that walked like men, he was learning a lot recently.

'Out here away from the cities the law doesn't apply the same way,' put in the Hawk.

'Well why not?' he asked.

'The king may rule the land in law but does he in practice? In reality the local Lords and Knights have the real power in the outlying regions such as here. Did you ever notice the power your father had in his city? He wasn't a king but no one questioned his authority, his orders brooked no question.'

'Can we find another way around, this place gives me shivers.'

'We'll be past soon enough then on and it won't take us long then to get back on our course, the road we want to head east is not far past.

'There's someone in two of those traps, old friend,' interrupted Jak.

Marauder had lost them. He cursed under his breath repeatedly. He had returned to the Fyord Bridge then headed to the scene were his quarry had fled into the forest after his attack, but he couldn't make sense of the tracks. His prey were smart, they were good. They knew they were being hunted and now they were wise to him. But what were they? One almost looked like a bird as it climbed across the rope. He pulled some of his quarrels out of a tree near where they had fled. No sign of blood to follow, the heavy rain hadn't helped him. No one had escaped his clutches before. Two more darts were on the floor, he retrieved them also. As he racked his brain on where they might now be headed a horrible screeching filled the air. It was the like sound of many lives stuck in a raging fire unable to escape it, a noise of torture and pain. The raptors, this could be the break he needed. The assassin ran from the cover of the trees and scanned the air for them. The screeching became louder and he soon spotted them north up the river. There was no mistaking the beasts, their long necks pushed through the air as they soared. Their mostly black feathers looked in stark contrast to the now blue morning sky. It was like looking at a cloud racing past, they were heading east and quickly past from view. Marauder wasted no time mounting his horse and following them. Raptors weren't sent out lightly somehow his lord had gotten wind of his expedition and sent the terrifying creatures in pursuit of his prey, too.

He was freezing. The heavy rain had refreshed him at first but now this chill would be his end. The lunatic in the next trap cursed loudly swinging it with all his might, but it wouldn't fall and he wouldn't break out. Braydon had almost tuned him out barely aware he was still there. He just sat with his knees against his chest hoping for a miracle. He didn't deserve to rot here. Then he saw movement. Yes, some folk were coming his way. One looked young and the other two were hooded. All were armed; as a military, well ex-military man that's something you notice quickly about folk. There was something strange about the hooded pair, too. The slighter of the two hooded figures slowed them. They had a small conversation it seemed then they carried on cautiously. The kid now pulled up his own hood.

He shouted out to them but no reply. Syzmon now noticed them too and yelled louder than ever, shaking his steel prison demanded yet also pleading to be freed.

'They're both men. Caged, from what I can see the traps they are in seem secure,' noted Chajak.

'Agreed we can continue, but put your hood up and ignore them both.' Remaining silent Austin was now carrying the Guardian's sword over his shoulders still wrapped up since they no longer had horses, he gripped it tightly behind his hip as he fell in line past Jak. The cat removed her swords spun them around in her hands then slammed the claws on the ends of the handles together and with a snap the two became one long weapon that she held low at her side. Hcur made no movement towards his own mace.

The sight of Jak's sword made Syzmon fall momentarily silent, the three walked quickly up the track maybe 40 feet from the gallows tree. Jak and Hcur made no effort to look at the caged men, but Austin couldn't help it. Now they could also see the path they wanted was not far off.

'Friends will you help a poor soldier whose hope is almost gone?' called out Braydon, with that Syzmon commenced his yelling all over again.

'We don't help criminals,' replied Austin before Hcur could stop him, he grabbed the boy by the shoulder and pushed him ahead a bit.

'You should not be so hasty to judge, friends, my punishment does not fit my crime, and will you not hear my tale?' he had to shout to be heard over the ranting from the next cage. He could hear Chajak's riposte well enough though.

'Neither your crime nor punishment are of consequence to us.' The cat didn't even turn to speak. Braydon wanted to say some more, but something caught his attention. A humming could be heard from the direction of the river, Hcur and Jak had noticed it too.

'That sound is growing, and I'm sure it's coming our way Hcur'

'What can it be?'

'It sounds like nothing I've heard before.'

Even Syzmon had stopped to listen, but he soon started again,

'It's the flying death,' he called out over and over, he looked at the three travellers, 'you need to get us out, the flying death will take us!' All searched the skies but nothing could be seen yet. Braydon thought for a moment then recalled something he had heard of long ago.

'Raptors,' he muttered as he recalled they also known to some as the flying death. 'Run while you can, I fear my companion here may be right Raptors are coming' he shouted.

'By the Phoenix were in trouble now,' said Hcur grabbing his mace and Shield still looking for the sound.

'Look to the west, the criminals are right,' Jak's keen eyesight had caught a glimpse at last. 'We're too far from good cover and that swarm is heading too fast.

The humming had become screeching and now even Austin could see the Raptors they were charging towards their position at breakneck speed, they swooped down low screaming trying to intimidate their foes. While they were known to all as Raptors their real name was Stymphalian birds, in addition to their deadly feathers they boasted talons sharper than razors and a beak that could pierce a soldier's breast plate.

'Take cover by that old gallows it's our only hope!' yelled Hcur.

'Free me and I can help, I'm a soldier,' pleaded Braydon. But the trio ignored his call. At the rotten gallows the Hawk kicked part of its wooden construction away and roughly threw Austin underneath its base. Both he and Jak had their weapons drawn waiting for their quarry.

The Raptors closed in fast, twenty of them in total, when they got close enough they flicked their wings and long black feathers shot out. The poisonous quills were razor sharp and could pierce light armour. They rained down indiscriminately not only on the trio but also the prisoners in the cages. The Cheetah spun and swung her swords so fast they became a blur, deflecting the deadly arrows the feathers that missed stuck fast in the wooden frame of the gallows or tree bark. A few lodged into Hcur's shield his mace proved to be no use for batting away the quills. Both Cheetah and Hawk had to throw back their hoods during the onslaught to see the enemy more clearly.

Braydon sighed with relief when one feather imbedded itself in the cage rather than his chest, a few more sailed uncomfortably close by. In the next cage Syzmon let out a horrifying scream then fell silent and slumped down never to move again. Two feathers had struck him one in the arm the other in the neck. His skin around the wounds turned black immediately as the poison entered his system.

'We can't keep this up, my friend, we will tire soon,' shouted Jak.

'Let us hope that they tire first then,' was his friend's reply. But both knew they needed to come up with a plan fast.

At Braydon's cage his fortunes took a turn for the better when by chance one of the deadly feathers cracked open the lock that was barring his escape. He fell through the bottom of his prison cell; he hit the dirt rolled and ran straight towards the trio of strangers. Hcur could see him coming but could do nothing without taking his focus away from the birds. Braydon made straight for the gallows under which Austin hid; he had noticed when they approached that the boy had a bow and quiver of arrows over his shoulder. Braydon yanked them off the boy who was too stunned to object. Austin held the sword tight, grateful he didn't try and grab it.

'I need to borrow these, lad' he said leaving the shelter with an arrow notched and ready to fire. Quickly aiming at the attacking Raptors he released the grip of the bowstring and a black bird fell from the sky. Then another was quickly dispatched.

This was the opening Jak needed she leapt at some of the evil attackers spinning in the air splitting her sword back into two she stretched her arms out looking almost like a propeller, a Raptor lost its wings to her blades another immediately lost its head. As she landed she brought her weapons to bear on a bird directly in front of her, cleaving the enemy into three.

The birds' attack stuttered under this opposition and two drew too close to Hcur with a back-handed swing he crushed one with his mace, drawing it back he smashed another into the dirt. The Hawk's weapon proved much more useful in attack rather than defence. Braydon had felled two more; searching the sky for another target he failed to notice a Raptor swooping in behind him, it flicked its wings and quills flew at the soldiers back but Hcur had seen it and hurled his shield to his defence. The shield flew through the air and blocked the feathers from hitting their target, Hcur charged the offending Raptor but it was too quick and took back to the sky.

Austin didn't know what to do, he wanted to help his companions just as the stranger was, but he remained rooted where he was and could only peer through cracks in the wood to see what was happening. He gripped the Guardian's sword tightly, but it was still wrapped up in its coverings. The thought of using it didn't cross his mind.

The Raptors sensing the tide was turning started to flee. Jak's swords had dispatched two more, as they left she took a dagger from her belt and tossed it at the closest to her, it hit between the bird's wings and it fell from the air. Braydon's last arrow did likewise to one more as they fled.

As soon as the Raptors had gone Hcur turned his focus to Braydon

'Stranger you have my friend's bow,' he said. Braydon lowered the bow and dropped it next to his feet.

'I no longer need it, don't look so wary I'm not your enemy, but tell me who are you?'

'We thank you for your help, but I have no intention of explaining anything to you,' said the Hawk curtly.

'You look like a man yet have the face of an eagle.' Austin emerged from his hiding place but the trio said no more to Braydon.

'I'm no eagle,' Hcur responded quietly he and Jak pulled up their hoods once more. 'Are you OK?' the hawk asked Austin.

'Yes I'm fine, what where they?'

'The flying death,' interrupted Braydon. 'Rumours suggest few have survived attack by Raptors and lived to tell it. You must be skilled warriors indeed.'

'And you are skilled with the bow I notice,' said Hcur turning back to Braydon briefly.

'They aren't sent out lightly; seldom have I heard of them attacking even the Royal Army, why would these pursue you? And yes I can fire bow as I formally served as an archer.'

'You're a military man and a criminal?' spat Jak. 'Just our luck'

'My punishment doesn't fit my crime; I was locked up for attacking my superior. He attacked a young woman I hit him to my cost and was made an example of. Don't mess with your commanding officers, but I don't regret my actions. My name is Braydon; again I ask who you are?'

'We are just three travellers, soldier, thanks once more for your help it is now time we continued our journey.'

'I have only heard of men like you in stories and may never come across your kind again, can you not tell my something more about yourselves?'

'We have no intention to,' interrupted Jak this time.

'I'm far from home and it seems there are forces about I know little of. May I join your company?'

'No chance,' spat Jak pointing her swords at him. 'Return to the town, someone there will help you.

'Tombstone's a ghost town, I won't find help there, by turning me away you may be sentencing me to death,' Braydon had a wry grin, Austin didn't believe he meant what he said.

'You draw conclusions from very few facts, archer,' said Hcur. 'I know little of why these Raptors attacked us and would doubt they would pursue you again. You may likely be safer to see the back of us.'

'How can we trust you?' asked Austin.

'Have I given you a reason not to?'

Austin looked at his friends. Before they could speak Braydon did.

'Let me show you some good faith while you discuss it.' He proceeded to start gathering all the arrows he could mostly by pulling them out of the carcasses of fallen Raptors, he even retrieved the knife Chajak hurled at one.

'I don't sense any deceit in him, Austin, but we don't need any more complications, we have a task to complete. Your father chose to send you with us to avoid it,' he nodded at the sword, 'being a temptation to others.'

'Can we leave someone in the wild with those creatures about, though? He did help us,' he said as he put his bow back over his shoulders.

'You're from a military family and look well on soldiers I understand that. But I'm certain he can look after himself look,' Braydon was now examining the arrows discarding any bent ones and sharpening the tips of the others with some flint he found.

As they turned to leave, though, Hcur noticed a bat hanging underneath the cell that Braydon had occupied not long before. The bird got the feeling that it was sizing him up before it flew quickly off to the western sky. Jak noticed it now, too.

'Is that a bat in these parts?' she said.

'And out at this time alone.' The Hawk added, he thought long over his next words. He recognised the signs of danger clearly, the bat was more than a bad omen it was an instrument of the Black Prince. His shoulders dropped slightly and he let slip a small sigh. 'It is clear we are no longer safe. We must now assume that Sinister will soon know of us, it is time to make haste.'

Braydon approached and returned the arrows to Austin before handing Jak her blade back, she snatched it without a word.

'The danger we are in is graver than I first feared, archer,' said Hcur. 'The Dark Lords spies are hunting us. And I would guess he now knows of you, too, it is probable he will hunt you also. We head east you can join us till you decide when and where it is you want to go.' Jak shook her head in disgust but held her tongue. She started back towards the path.

'Why would the Dark Lord send Raptors after you?' Braydon asked.

'I'm not explaining that now, later maybe. Come if you want we're going now, Austin, let's go.' Hcur led Austin after the cat. Braydon stood in his rags hands upon his hips, he had nowhere else to go, but did he want to get entangled with the mess. There was no choice really, his interest was already piqued. He briskly walked after them.

Chapter VII: Deadly Pursuit

Venom spotted her next target easier than she had expected, Marauder was charging east. She swooped down and flew near his galloping horse, sighting her he pulled up and the dragon landed nearby.

'The Dark Prince knows you pursue someone,' she said flashing her teeth. She was a menacing figure even to her allies.

'That's what I do,' he said, not bringing himself to meet her glance.

'He desires to know who. Sent me all the way out here to find you'

'I don't know yet, but they caught my interest also they have something I desire to see though I don't know why.'

'The Raptors have been sent to deal with them, so you'll be able to pick the bones of what's left.' She then froze and cocked her head slightly. Her eyes narrowed. 'Speaking of the Raptors they return.'

Marauder looked to the skies but even his keen sight could see nothing yet. The Dragon grabbed him roughly by his arms and flew him to the peak of a nearby hill despite his protests.

'You won't need the horse anymore,' she hissed.

Venom could see the Raptors in the distance she let out a massive roar and flashed her wings. She then dropped Marauder to the ground then landed herself. Marauder now could see the birds; they flew in fast and landed on the hill but none came too close, even the deadly Raptors feared the great dragon.

'Only seven are here skulking now on this hillside yet twenty left the citadel' the birds responded to Venom in their own language all screeching wildly yet had heads hung low and where backing away further.

'I can't recall your kind failing before. It's a great shame.' She looked back to Marauder who recognised failure and gave her a nod. As she turned back to the Raptors a huge flame spouted from inside her incinerating the birds. The creeping death had to turn away from the screeching, twenty had become seven and seven became none. Almost instantly all that remained of them was charcoal ashes amongst the scorched earth.

'Those you pursue still live, their attack failed, just as yours did,' snarled Venom.

'Take me to them then they won't be underestimated again. I'll end this trek of theirs.'

'Perhaps I should help this time; they've clearly got something about them to have survived two challenges.'

'No, they're my pursuit I'll deal with them you need to keep to the Dark Prince's orders.

'Their number may have increased, the Raptors hinted someone helped your quarry.'

'It matters not, I've taken down greater numbers before.'

'But few with the skill of these. They also told me that two were a Hawk and a Leopard or perhaps Cheetah of the old race. You haven't dealt with their kind before.' This news interested Marauder.

'I suspected one was a bird when I caught a glimpse of them over the Sovereign.' He looked to the distance. 'It seems I'll get to test myself against creatures from the past then. I intend to see to it that none of them has a future. You may as well take me to them it'll save time but then follow your instructions, go to the Ridgeway, they're my prey.'

Very well then let's go.' She again grabbed Marauder roughly and took to the skies.

Chajak was still annoyed at Braydon expanding the trio, Hcur insisted he stay if the enemy caught him and learned more of them it would be ill tidings for them the Hawk argued. Braydon and Austin walked together for a while Austin eager to learn about the Archer and any news he may have of elsewhere in Ridgedale, but the Archer revealed little of himself other than he was a loyal soldier not that long ago.

After a while the rocky scenery they crossed slowly turned into grasses as they headed towards the plains of Hazeldene. The plains were rather dull Austin thought to himself after all the sights and action they had seen previously. Mostly long grass but dandelions, gypsophila, thistles, daisies and buttercups mixed together contently in places also. And the very occasional hazel tree after which the area was named. It took the group and day a morning to travel the plains. Far in the distance a great wood sprung up almost from nowhere, signalling the end of the plains as the wooded valley dipped away from the Hazeldene. Beyond that could be seen the mountains that formed the border to the forbidden lands. When they stopped Austin much to his annoyance now had to contend with Braydon offering advice as Jak continued to tutor him.

They settled for the night on the plains, they had slowly gotten to know Braydon some on the trek from Tombstone but he was very cautious with what he revealed to them. He was more interested in finding out about them. Jak and Hcur refused to say anything about themselves to him and Jak had said nothing to him whatsoever all day. Braydon surprisingly knew little news of Argentum Austin thought, he knew of the troubles but had no idea how bad things were. Braydon explained this as he had spent most of his career on patrol in the east and the officers didn't report much down to his level.

'Can I even ask where you are heading?' he asked as they ate supper. Both Hawk and Cheetah just stared back at him with the hint of a smile from one and total annoyance from the other. Austin had revealed a lot of his background to Braydon but Hcur kept him from saying anything about the sword. That is until Braydon mentioned the package Austin carried.

'Why do you keep your sword wrapped up like a parcel?' Hcur and Jak noticeably shifted at this.

'What makes you think it's a sword?' was all Austin could think to say.

'Well look at the size of it, what else can it be.' The soldier met Austin's gaze. 'And the way you carry it, gingerly, as if it's dangerous, yet close like it's important.' No one spoke so he continued. 'To me a sword is a sign of honour and military prestige. It shouldn't be smuggled about, you should carry it as a symbol of strength.

'You guess correctly it's a sword. It's important to the boy and we're taking him to safety.' Huffed Hcur, 'Nothing else is important. Drop the matter or we'll part ways sooner rather than later.' They ate in silence for a few moments. Austin was sure he could trust Braydon his father had told him to listen to his instincts and his gut told him Braydon was OK.

'Is it the Wyrm? That's the sword the Captain of the Silver Tower wields isn't it?' asked the archer presently.

'My father would never part with the Wyrm. It was my grandfather's I think.'

'But surely it would pass to you; I would like to see the blade that has cleaved the necks of a thousand Goblyns.'

'That many hey!' chuckled Hcur.

'It must be a great number and how it is held with all those barbs is another marvel. The Wyrm is magic.' Declared Braydon.

'Leather and chain mail, nothing magic about it,' answered Austin. 'Your glove has to be thick but free enough to use your hand effectively, also there is a knack to where you position you're hand on the hilt. My father still needs the *Wyrm that bites its own tail*. If I'm lucky I may inherit it one day if I'm very lucky that day will not be anytime soon.'

'Right no more tip toeing around here's the situation Archer. We do carry a sword with us,' interrupted Chajak, Hcur and Austin looked at her to see where she was going. 'I'm getting weary of minding what we say so I'll tell you what our purpose is. But first let me tell you that if you betray us by attempting to steal it or by another means, one of us,' she nodded at the Hawk 'but most likely I will kill you.' She pointed her thumb at herself. This was the most Jak had spoken to Braydon so far; he looked hard at her and could tell she was deadly serious. And from what he had seen of them he knew this was no idle threat none the less he agreed eager to learn more.

'The boy carries the Guardian's sword, or Phoenix sword you may also know it by. Do you know it?' Braydon stared intently at her for a moment then slowly nodded. 'We are taking it to Aurum, not with the men fleeing the silver city for fear it may end up in the wrong hands.' Austin felt it an appropriate time to reveal the Blade. He held it up for Braydon to see in all its glory. The early moonlight shone brightly on its silver form. Braydon stretched out a hand slowly as if to take it, but Austin drew the weapon back closer to him, Braydon's hand lowered. He didn't notice, so focused was he on the Silver sword, but both Jak and Hcur moved their hands closer to their own weapons when he did this.

'It can't be put into words how magnificent that sword is.' He finally spoke. 'The sword that killed twenty dragons!

I'm trying to recall the verse; shouldn't the unveiling of the sword crown a new king?'

'That is correct and that is why we are taking it to the Golden city,' said Hcur. The Old King has failed not only your people but ours, too. If your kingdom falls ours will be next.'

'So who will you hand it to?' asked Braydon.

'Someone who reveals themselves to be worthy,' was the Hawk's reply.

'That's it?' laughed the archer. 'You're going to march into a city of many people, soldiers and bureaucrats and hope one of them will take the sword because he smiles nicely at you?'

'*That* is not what I said.'

'I could take it, I could lead our kingdom against the dark forces' said Braydon standing 'I've already given my adult life to serving Ridgedale, who would be better I ask?' Jak unsheathed her swords from her back and laid them in front of her as if to say calm yourself, but he ignored the sign.

'I could take it' he repeated'

'Not on your life' the cat answered with a steel look in here amber eyes.

'This is why we didn't go with everyone else,' said Austin with frustration.

'Many will want it, you're the proof but not everyone has the ability to rule,' said Hcur. 'You're too easily tempted by the promise of its power.'

'Then I will prove myself to you all.' He sat back down. 'Always I felt I had more to offer my country. I will aid you in any way I can to see your task completed. Put it away Austin I won't take it from you, but perhaps when we get to Aurum you will present it to me.'

As they neared the end of the Hazeldene far to the left Austin could see a hill sticking out like a plough into the flat countryside. It was covered almost entirely with trees even its very steep sloped side which looked south across the plains. Unseen at this distance was Hayden's Keep, a small village at the bottom of the hill while just about visible at the top was a small castle with the same name and occupied by the chief of the region whose name escaped him. It was fine warm and clear barely a cloud could be seen above, it was pleasant walking weather.

Just before the tree line Jak spotted three men riding a cart heading north slightly. A single horse was pulling it, the cart was open and several boars were loaded in the back. Jak and Hcur pulled their hoods up to hide their faces even at this distance; Austin was glad he didn't have to pull his up in under this sun. He thought they must look a rabble, two hooded strangers and a man in rags. The four of them slowed their pace and fell into single file Jak seemed anxious that the men in the cart would surely spot them she suggested they pause several times. If the folk on the wagon did catch sight of them then they paid no great attention much to the cheetah's relief.

'The boars are good in these parts I hear,' said Braydon 'that wagon will most likely be headed back to Aurum.' Hcur agreed, he knew the king's men hunted here. The wagon was never that close and was well up the track away from them by the time they came to the trees.

The wood they entered was dense, tall wide trees almost blocked the afternoon sun from view, even though the path was clear and wide. Austin shivered slightly, the dark green wood seemed damp to him he wished to be back out on the open of the Hazeldene. The four travelled for a while in silence when Jak stopped them shaking her head in frustration.

'There are two more men up ahead just over that dip.'

'Are you sure?' asked Braydon. None of them needed or wanted another encounter with the green assassin. Austin had mentioned the man who had pursued them while they travelled. He had only heard whispers of this unusual weapon the assassin used until now. 'I'm unarmed friends.' He added.

'Here take my bow.' Austin took off his quiver of arrows and handed them both to the archer. Braydon immediately put a bow to the string.

'Let's see who they are shall we, it's unusual for your kind to enter this forest,' said Hcur. 'Jak circle around to the left we'll keep going on slowly.' Without missing a beat the Cheetah leapt silently away and disappeared into the bush.

'Keep your eyes sharp we out number them, but we don't know their intentions,' Hcur said to Austin. Austin took out the Phoenix sword and held it ready, the first time he had done so. He liked the feel of it, it gave him a confidence. Braydon's earlier talk of wanting it increased his own desire to keep it so he may as well use it he decided. Hcur who usually led with his shield rather than his mace decided to take no chances now. His great weapon was now gripped tightly in his feathered right hand. 'It's odd to chance upon any folk out here and luck has been our enemy of late.' He whispered.

They could hear voices as they crept up on the men. Why they were here Austin couldn't guess but they clearly didn't expect anyone else to be around. Braydon and Hcur had also gathered as much. They saw a covered cart first it wasn't very big with a dark green canvas cover and it had no beast to tow it. Two men sat drinking near a small fire just past it.

'Bandits.' Whispered Braydon. Hcur nodded in agreement.

'We can go around they won't notice we've been here.'

'But on the other hand they may have some supplies we can use.'

'Drawing attention to ourselves is a grief we don't need.' The hawk said firmly. Braydon nodded again and lowered his bow slightly. Austin without looking took a slow step backwards at this news and a large twig snapped loudly under his boot. The bandits looked up quickly reaching for their weapons but before they could stand Chajak burst through the bushes behind them swords ready. She placed one each under the chins of the two men before they knew what had happened.

Both looked at the cat in stunned amazement as Braydon Austin and Hcur also left their cover.

'Animals' cried one looking at Jak and Hcur, his voice was a mixture of hate and fear. He had thick shaggy hair that almost covered his eyes, both dressed in green and brown rags.

'Who are you?' whimpered the other. He was smaller than his companion and clearly very afraid.

'Jak lower your blades,' said the hawk.

'They went for theirs when they heard you, you were careless,' she hissed in return.

'We would go for our own if someone snuck up on us, friend.'

Jak took a few steps back but she did not lower her swords. Hcur turned to face the bandits. 'Few venture in these parts what is your business here?' The bigger of the two answered;

'Freaks! You dare to question us!' What right do you have to do that?' was the snarled answer. Austin couldn't decide if he was bold or stupid.

'You're very jittery. We were passing through and we chance upon you,' said Braydon. 'As my friend here said it's rare to see others in this area.'

'Our business here is none of yours.'

'We can't let them go now they've seen us, they may alert our enemies,' decided Chajak.

'They may be miscreants but they've done us no harm,' put in Hcur.

'So what do we do?' demanded Braydon. But the shaggy haired Bandit made his move while they pondered this. A knife fell from his sleeve to his hand; he slashed it towards them all wildly. Only Jak stood her ground both swords now trained on him, the others stepping back slightly. In the commotion the smaller of the two ran for his life.

'Enough of this' yelled Braydon as quick as a flash he raised his bow and loosed an arrow which hit his target square in the chest. The shaggy haired bandit fell and would never rise again. 'What of the other?'

Jak turned to chase but Hcur spoke up.

'Let him go. He can't do us any harm.'

'He could tell the enemy of our whereabouts,' protested the Cheetah roaring.

'Why would he? And if by chance he does he knows nothing of us or our task.' Jak and Braydon finally nodded in agreement. While the group had no official leader all respected the old Hawk and his decisions even those who had only just got to know him.

Braydon turned his attention to the covered wagon while Jak noticed a small bag near were the bandits had been sitting. In it were several gold coins which she quickly pocketed. Something had immediately caught Braydon's eye in the wagon. Amongst all the loot, of which most was worthless, could be seen a sword. This treasure stood out from everything else like an elephant in a field of sheep. The sword was long longer than any other blade Austin had seen. Gold in colour and a silver blade with a golden circle around the hilt that would just about allow four hands to grip the handle inside it. It was so long it couldn't be hung around the waist as the tip would surely drag across the floor. The blade was about an inch and a half wide until near the tip where it slowly started arching out on one side to a point and there it arched quickly back to the tip itself. As Braydon reached out for it he saw some markings on its side, Hcur translated them as sword of the moon in the old runes of Viridis.

'It's magnificent,' The archer gasped.

'Mine's better,' put in an affronted Austin. They all just looked at him. It was so very different from the Phoenix sword, it was extravagant and bold, the Guardian's sword was elegance itself, simple beauty.

'It might not be the Guardian's sword but it is damn fine. I'm claiming this one my friends as you're already armed and it seems our friends weren't bowmen.'

'I prefer my mace, archer,' stated Hcur.

'I have two of my own but I won't deny I would desire that blade,' said Jak as she joined them at the wagon, Braydon passed it to her and she spun it around and sliced the air. The blade disappeared in a blur such was her speed. She returned it to Braydon. 'A good weapon indeed.'

There was nothing else in the wagon of use to them save for some old clothes which just about fit Braydon. He didn't know how clean the previous owner may have been but decided they were better than his own rags. No scraps of food were around so they decided to carry on. As they left Braydon tore strips from the wagon's cover and strategically tied them to his new sword so he could carry it over his shoulder.

Venom slowly circled the skies above the Hazeldene high above Marauder who searched for traces of his quarry. The assassin had lost the tracks of those he chased, there were four tracks leaving the carcasses of the Raptors confirming what the now dead creatures had suggested. But in the long grasses it was tougher to find a trails which Marauder had never struggled with before. They certainly often marched single file and it became harder to find out where they may have gone. There were a few possibilities, if they were heading to the Golden City they may have gone north at the end of the plains believing they had at last lost their pursuit. If they went south they would have soon needed a boat; they were nearing the Sapphire Sea here. His hunch said they carried on east into the trees towards lands he had never tread. High above the dragon called down.

'There's a cart northwards.'

'They may have seen something let's go and ask.' Venom swooped down and grabbed his comrade and raced towards the wagon. The men in the cart saw them approached and took flight as fast as they could spurring there horse on but it was no use she was on them in no time. Dropping Marauder just before them she let out a huge burst of flame above the wagon then smashed into it side on sending it crashing onto its side. The horse pulling it scrambled back to its feet only to be incinerated by Venom along with the first of the passengers getting to their feet.

'Mercy mercy we've done you no harm!' pleaded the next man to his feet. The third stayed on his knees.

'We're not your enemy,' he said trembling. They both wore a simple pale uniform the man on his knees had a bushy moustache. Marauder approached with his crossbow trained on the man standing.

'Not my enemy? I'll come back to that, firstly have you seen four men on the Hazeldene while you crossed?'

'What wait, yes, yes not long ago,' stumbled one trying his best to recall.

'They went into the trees I think,' cried the other.

'Sure yes the trees definitely went into the trees. Odd looking bunch all covered up in this sun,' The first stuttered.

'Thanks that's what we needed to know.' The assassin didn't lower his weapon 'one more thing where are you headed?'

'Aurum, Aurum' they cried in unison. They fell backwards both with darts in the throat barely before they had finished their answer.

'Then you are my enemy,' was Marauder's cold response. 'They are continuing east as I thought, the creatures must be taking the men to their own lands. We must intercept them quickly. Venom raised her great wings and headed back to the skies Marauder in her talons but not before she had torched the cart and two bodies first.

At last the foursome came to the gate of the forgotten lands. No man had passed this way and through to the Goodyson canyon and the lands beyond in generations. They had been slowly marching down into a valley on the only path in these parts which was now seldom trod. The woods eventually gave way to a large clearing and the path continued to a great waterfall. It must have been eighty feet wide crescent in shape and it thundered down in to a lake on the edge of which the path stopped.

'Where do we go now?' asked Austin.

'The path goes straight on, young one,' replied Hcur.

'The path stops just ahead of us by the lake,' Austin said confused, Chajak chuckled at this. Hcur answered again.

'The waterfall that you see is the doorway.'

'Wait till you see what's behind,' added the cat. 'Even you will be amazed, Archer.'

'We'll see.'

'What's behind it then?' said Austin as they made their way around the lake to the waterfall's edge. Nearing the flowing torrents he could feel the cool spray on his face it invigorated and refreshed him. Jak who was leading the way stopped just short of the fall, turned to him and said,

'Come and find out.' With that she stepped through the downpour. Austin could just about make her out on the other side.

'Oh great we're going to get soaked,' Braydon moaned but he went through the falls none the less. The great old bird looked at Austin and smiled and gave a nod in the direction of the water. The boy pulled his hood up put the Phoenix sword under his cloak and ran through the curtain of water. The other side was wondrous. To say the cavern was vast would be an understatement. Looking past where his companions were shaking the water off he could see walls that shone silver here copper there that side was gold greens and blues also. A wide path twisted and dropped slightly ahead and then it followed the stream which flowed in from the waterfall's lake. Daylight could just be seen a mile or so away at the far side where the stream headed. Mighty stalactites hung from the caverns ceiling in places stalagmites reached up to great them. As they walked they saw evidence of old fires.

'The stream here leads to the canyon. Said Hcur. 'It's one of the Goodyson's many tributaries. We are not far from the Aerie now will camp in here tonight and tomorrow we'll enjoying the hospitality of my people.

'Was that the falls of Lowan?' asked Braydon.

'The falls of what?' said Austin.

'That is one of many names for it; I know it as simply as the Curtain,' replied Hcur.

'Wasn't Lowan one of the first kings of Ridgedale?' asked Austin.

'He was, lad, and legend has it he stood in that lake and commanded the waterfall to stop flowing,' Braydon said with a gesture back to the falls.

'Really, well what happened?' Austin asked unsure that anyone could be that deluded.

'He drowned,' Braydon answered simply.

'I don't believe that myth; it is a tale that has taken and added to over the ages,' put in Hcur with a shake of his head.

'I don't know if it's true or not,' added Braydon, 'but I do think all legends have some truths in them.'

'I'm convinced it's true,' was all that Jak would say on the matter.

After supper around a small campfire Braydon finally opened up a little to his companions, as they settled down for the night he told them he was from a little hamlet at the northern most point of the Ridge mountains where they met the sea. It was a quaint little place the small houses all made from wood and most of the inhabitants were fisherman. He joined the army when he was about Austin's age a little underage but the army rarely asked questions. He had always been a good archer and enjoyed hunting as a boy and took and developed those skills as a soldier, his skills with the bow soon set him apart from rest of his peers. He resented the fact he couldn't progress up the ranks only the noblemen or other important citizens got to the highest positions in the army of Rigdedale, men like Braydon had to be happy with what they had.

He showed them his skills in the morning after their breakfast using Austin's bow. He set a log against the cavern wall and quickly fired three shots all hit the target all within millimetres. Retrieving the arrows he fired again this time while striding across the cave as before they landed so very close together and practically in the holes he had previously made. Even Chajak was impressed by this with her cat instincts she was a good shot but nowhere near as accurate as Braydon.

'I've the eyes of a hawk,' the archer laughed. Hcur chuckled and shook his head.

'It's funny isn't it?' said Braydon as they prepared to set off.

'What is?' asked Austin.

'You say you have the Guardian's sword and I believe you no questions asked. I mean it's funny that I don't doubt that three strangers I've only just met have the sword, even though there have been a few impostors and forgeries over the years claiming the very same thing.'

'That is because the Phoenix herself made it and when it comes to the Firebird there are never any doubts,' answered Hcur. 'The sword is the embodiment of her spirit her soul and her strength, all that is good about her.'

'How was it in Argentum for so long without anyone knowing?' Braydon asked the bird.

'I can't help you there as I only found out about it just before we started our quest.'

'Do you know, Austin?' The archer questioned.

'No I found out the same night, the night we left. Father said it had been handed down since my great grandfather I think, so, well, that's over a hundred years, but how long the Lords of the Tower had it before then I could not answer.'

The city of Eagles Aerie chief dwelling of all the great birds was located on the side of the Great Chasm. The Chasm was also known as the Goodyson or forbidden canyon, depending on who you asked, and through which the mighty river Goodyson flowed. The canyon snaked through the land for some miles it would be impassable save for the few wooden bridges traversing it. The most direct way to the city was to actually cross it twice via the bridges; to follow it round its bends would make any journey a very long trek. The chasm walls were a browny-red stone. Yellow flowers with green leaves clung on in places reaching out for the sunlight, and underneath the deep blue waters of the Goodyson flowed strong adding more colour to the scene.

The first rope bridge didn't look at all safe to Braydon but Chajak and Hcur assured him it was in fact. He looked at Austin who just shrugged.

'This old bridge was here before you were, archer, and will last after you're gone,' chided the hawk.

'That's what I'm worried about; it looks rotten.'

'It's fine, I've crossed more times than I can count,' replied Hcur.

'And the drop isn't that far,' scoffed Jak. Looking over the side Braydon estimated the drop must have been at least thirty five feet long. And it was sharp looking rocks underneath at first the Goodyson didn't pass below till a third of the bridge was crossed.

'Come the city's not far, respite awaits us,' said the Hawk again.

Austin looked forward to seeing where Hcur hailed from and followed eagerly ignoring the steep drop over the canyon. The bridge was at least seventy feet long, but it was sturdy, it didn't rock or sway much with three of them on it. Shortly Braydon started to cross also. It was made with thick rope and heavy woods and he held on to both sides tightly.

Hcur, Jak and Austin had just reached halfway when a giant flame fell from the sky before them hitting the far side of the bridge like a thunderbolt. The bridge rocked and Austin fell on his back only Jak remained on both feet. They looked back to see a huge black dragon in the sky. It landed on the bank behind them and let out a huge screech. More fire erupted from it into the sky. Just in front of the beast was a man clad in green. The same person who had attacked them over the sovereign. He charged towards them while the dragon watched intently. Braydon's fear left him as his training took over, he drew his new sword and charged back. Austin drew the Guardian's sword and Jak did likewise with her own blades, Hcur only hoisted his shield from his shoulders and pushed the others towards Marauder, who seemed the lesser of two evils. There was no way to pass the fire that now raged on the far side. The bridge was burning and damaged critically.

The dragon's eyes glinted when she saw Austin's weapon, but Venom failed to recognise it and took flight again; she had set up the Marauder's prey like fish in a barrel. For good measure she torched the bank around the burning side of the bridge, and roared again confident the assassin could finish the job. She soared back to her master while the red flames flicked up into the blue sky.

Jak was shoving Austin back the way they had come Hcur on her tail. The fire roared on the far side of the canyon, the burning bridge would soon give way. Marauder now aimed his weapon on his end of the bridge but to his everlasting frustration it failed him, he gave a heavy knock and tried shooting again to no avail. Unbelievable timing, luck rides with them he thought, he unsheathed a short sword just as Braydon neared. He took everything in around him, all his targets were armed, four opponent's four swords a bow a mace, unused, and one shield. Then he and Braydon clashed blades, the shoulder high sides of the bridge prevented larger swings from either man. Both men instead tried using hard elbows and knees on their foe. As the three neared them Jak with incredible agility leapt onto the high rope over Austin and ran past Braydon then sprung down on Marauder planting her right foot square on his chest. He collapsed on the wooden rungs while she landed on her feet, just as she was about to bring her swords down on him, though, there was a loud snap and the rope bridge shook violently. All were knocked off balance and were holding on in sheer desperation, on his knees Austin looked back only one rope was now fastened to the far side and that too was burning.

A fall now seemed certain Austin feared and their quest would be over and more than likely their lives also. He also didn't know what to do with the sword, hold it tight or let it go? Would his hands be better served grabbing the bridge for safety and balance? He decided the sword was more important, it was the most important thing in the world to him now.

'Come on we need to get off the bridge!' he cried.

He and Braydon managed to leap over their fallen foe while he was still stunned from Jak's boot and scramble off the bridge. The Creeping Death attempted to grab the boy but Jak seized his wrist instead, then she whacked his head hard with the butt of her sword. Thinking he was subdued she, too, fled over him to safety. As Hcur manoeuvred past him, though Marauder tackled the Hawk, grabbing both his legs rolling over and thrusting his shoulder into the back of the bird's knees. Hcur tried kicking the assailant off, but he held firm. He squeezed Hcur's legs like a vice as if his life depended on it. Jak was now safe with the others, but seeing what was happening started to go to her friend's aid, but it was too late, the last burning rope gave up its fight on the other end and the whole bridge dropped from that side.

The strong wood foundation was pulled and groaned under the stress but against all hope held firm on their side. After smashing across the canyon wall the bridge now looked more like a rope ladder and it partly draped itself across the chasm's floor for good measure. Against the odds Hcur and the attacker had somehow held on. Marauder now released Hcur's legs and tried to climb up level with the Hawk, punching and clawing at him as he did so. Hcur was now weapon less; his great mace had fallen from his grip and now lay on the canyon floor below. Both his hands held on tight to the battered structure, but he knew just how to stop any more punches.

He let go of the bridge and grabbed Marauder who didn't expect this turn of events. They both fell several feet down the bridge before being able to stop themselves by grasping the rungs once more. Hcur now kicked at his slender foe a few rungs below him and he dropped a few more feet. Hcur now started to climb carefully back up the bridge, Marauder gripped his boot just as the plank he was holding gave out. Hcur looked down at his foe desperately clinging onto his foot for dear life. He swung his leg out into the void and brought Marauder crashing back into the bridge. The stranger held still on.

'It's you or I, freak,' he called up. Hcur swung out his leg again but still his enemy held firm.

'It's you then.' Cried the Hawk and with his free foot he kicked the fingers wrapped around his boot. At last the grip was released and the assassin plummeted. He landed square on his back not far from the Goodyson's edge and remained still. Austin peering over from the top gave a huge sigh of relief. After regaining his composure Hcur climbed the rungs and when he neared the top Braydon and Jak hauled him up.

'It would seem we're going the long way round,' he jested, but none of his companions could muster a laugh.

As the four companions continued on their way to the Aerie the Assassin once known as Kayden stirred. He wanted to sit up but all he could manage was to roll on to his side. A few feet away from him was a mace, he crawled over to it when his strength and wind at last returned. As far as he could tell nothing was broken. He gripped the mace and used it to scramble to his feet. His own weapons were close by, he gathered them and made his way to the remains of the rope bridge. They had eluded him again, no one had evaded him once yet alone twice. He shook his head and bit his lower lip hoping to shake off the pain of his back.

He had to continue after them, there was something about the way the boy held on to that sword. He didn't hold it like a weapon he carried it like a treasure. Marauder liked swords and the images of power they invoked. He had taken many from his victims over the years, and his collection was now huge, they lined the walls of his chambers back in Civitas Acerbus. He often dreamt that he could use one as his own but he knew they weren't ideal in his line of work so he continued to use the crossbow and a short blade he could more easily conceal. The boy's hilt was very interesting, even if they had not fled the Silver City under such intrigue he would have pursued them for it. He didn't even glimpse it clearly but it had drawn his attention, he wanted to see it now. He needed to. As he started climbing up something in the back of his mind bothered him. When he reached the top he threw the mace over first and a small engraving of an eagle on it caught his eye. He knew now what was bothering him. He almost could not believe it. He knew what the sword was. The mythical bird the sword was hers, it was *the* sword. He had to have it.

Hcur hurried the others along the winding path that led along the side of the canyon. The sooner they reached the Aerie the better.

'So this guy was the one who attacked you before?' asked Braydon as they went.

'Yes and he has followed us many miles,' replied the Hawk. 'All the way from Argentum I would guess.'

'Then he knows of the sword, why else would he chase you across the kingdom?' said the archer.

'That's impossible,' Austin added 'apart from we four no one else knows of the sword save my father.'

'Then Sinister's army tortured information of the sword out of him.' Suggested Braydon. Austin stopped he looked crestfallen and gazed out across the ravine. He missed his father so much and had no news of him, would he have been able to defend Argentum all this time? He had tried not to think of his father's fate to put it from his mind; he longed for news but that was out of the question here in the wilderness. The others stopped and Hcur put an arm around the boy.

'I'm not so sure about that, Braydon,' he said 'I think our Phantom followed us from the Silver City almost immediately, the city still stood when we left, there's no way Arian would have been defeated so quickly, if he has been defeated at all.' He gave Austin a reassuring look. 'He can't have known of the sword when he started his pursuit.'

'Then why does he follow us?' asked Austin.

'He's a servant of the Dark Prince, what other reason does he need,' said Jak stepping close to the edge of the canyon she sniffed the air for a moment then lowered her head. 'You're not going to believe this.' She uttered looking back at them.

Jak waited on the pass for the pursuit to arrive. He could only follow them further by going through me first she decided. She had chosen this spot carefully the tall cliff wall on one side the steep drop on the other, no way past without going through me she thought. While contemplating his arrival she sat crossed legged resting against a thin tree which hung out at a slight angle over the ravine. Presently her ears picked up and she heard the faint steps coming closer, then he came into view. Clad all in green it was certainly the same assailant who attacked them on the sovereign and again that morning. She drew her swords and snapped the hilts together, slowly she spun the weapon around with her wrists swapping it from hand to hand. He had seen her now and drew his own weapon aiming it at her; she didn't recognise it but was prepared for him now.

The weapon kicked back slightly a small projectile accelerated toward her. The spinning blades became a blur and she swung at the quarrel as it headed to her torso. A spark on the swords and the dart ended up in the tree by the edge.

Her enemy looked dumbfounded that's never happened to him before she correctly guessed.

The weapon kicked back two more times and again she blocked the shots, one hitting the cliff the other deflected into the abyss. He cursed and pierced her, but this time only with his sharp dark eyes. He charged at her tossing his weapon aside and Hcur's mace also, drawing his small sword. When he was a few feet away she rushed him, too. Steel clashed on steel. Her opponent was skilled but no match for her, but then he caught her unawares. After having a blow parried he used his momentum to roll backwards and threw a handful of dirt in her face. With Jak momentarily blinded he tackled her hard driving her into the ground she dropping her sword in the process. He had more strength than his slender frame suggested only after taking some stiff punches was she able to kick him off. Grabbing his blade again he began slashing at her; Jak was too quick for him though easily avoiding his swings. She charged him this time grabbing his wrist with one paw and his throat with the other, again they hit the ground. Quick as a flash with his free hand he fumbled the dirt and found what he needed, he smashed the back of her head with a large stone. She rolled off him stunned and regaining his feet he kicked at her savagely a few times than dragged her to her feet.

Holding the cat by the scruff of her neck and her waistline he ran her towards the ravine and threw her towards it. Jak pushed off him changing her direction slightly, she couldn't stop her forward momentum and instead used it to target the tree she leant on earlier. With both arms she grabbed at it and swung herself all the way around its trunk right over the drop below. She flew right back at her enemy feet first and landed both of them hard on his chest. He was knocked off his feet and somersaulted backwards landing his stomach. She retrieved her sword and separated the blades, Marauder had barely gotten to his knees.

'Why are you pursuing us?' she growled putting the blades across his neck.

'I won't answer to you, a freak of nature.' He wouldn't look up at her.

'And who do you answer to?' she demanded pressing the swords on his flesh 'tell me now or answer to no one ever again.'

'I serve the Dark Prince' he met her stare, 'reveal one thing for me and I'll speak.' He was trying to buy time, Jak knew, but he would do very well to escape his predicament.

'I'm asking the questions here assassin, not you.'

'You carry the sword?'

'What sword?'

'The legend, the Guardian's …' He had barely finished his sentence when Jak flung her arms wide apart, blood now stained the swords she held. Marauder's head rolled off his shoulders across the dirt track and over the precipice.

Chapter VIII: Eagles Aerie

Hcur had the others slow their pace while they waited for Chajak to catch up. He was made of stern stuff this man, even Braydon acknowledged that. The possibility existed of course that Jak wouldn't return and that the pursuit would continue, but Hcur had known her a long time, he could see the fire in her eyes. She wanted to be rid of him once and for all, and she was right he had to be taken care of. They trudged round the precipice in silence. Braydon was sulking as he wanted to go with her, he himself was annoyed Jak had gone as soon they would be at his home, and the attacker would not escape his from people. But Jak would not be told she wanted to wait for him, even Braydon knew she blamed herself for his coming so far after them.

A bird called from up ahead. It was a faint call Braydon and Austin missed it but Hcur didn't. He immediately motioned for the others to halt. The Hawk called out in his native tongue and a reply returned swiftly. Presently a figure dropped from a tree ahead bearing a resemblance to Hcur, save for his feather which were grey and white in colour. His beak was much shorter than Hcur's and mostly grey, his eyes were small and dark.

'Friends this is Colm the Falcon.'

'You vouch for these folk Hcur?' he said approaching.

'I do, we've been on quite an expedition together. I trust them completely.'

'I'm Braydon formerly of the army of Ridgedale and this is Austin son of Arian of Argentum.

'Welcome then, friends of Hcur.' Colm extended his feathered hand to greet them. 'I trust that your old companion the Cheetah is with you also. She follows you around the ridge.' The trio all let out a sigh of relive at this news.

'She had something to take care of; we'll wait for her here.'

'As you wish. You're going to the nest?'

'We seek shelter there for now.'

'Very well I'll send word of your coming.' The Falcon turned to leave. 'Nice to meet you all, perhaps we will break bread in the Aerie later, until then I've duties to return to.' They all bid him farewell. Austin watched as he left, Colm whistled out and a sparrow presently landed on his right shoulder. They seemed to talk then the little sparrow took flight.

'Can you talk to other birds then Hcur? Not just your own kind,' he asked.

'Not all but many we can talk to yes, mostly here in this region. Colm has just sent word to the Aerie of our arrival.'

'How long was he up ahead waiting for us?' asked Braydon.

'He wasn't up *there* very long, but he has been watching us for some time. It's his sentry duty today so very little will happen around the canyon today that he won't know about.'

At last Jak caught them up. She said nothing as she neared but her eyes told everything. Braydon went to speak to her but Hcur gestured with for him not too. She walked straight past them pausing only to hand Hcur his Mace. Austin just shrugged as he carried on Braydon followed, too. The Hawk thought for a moment and set off also.

It was a remarkable sight there was no doubt. The Aerie was staggering. The whole structure was tethered to the rock wall by a giant collection of thick vines. The city was really a collection of large timber chambers connected by smaller wooden corridors or rope bridges. Each chamber or room was carefully crafted to fit the white chasm wall. Many of the larger chambers were beautiful, with ornate carvings into the wooden frames and balconies that looked out into the huge void. It had little colour just the natural light textures of the wood used, and the sandy shade of the ropes. It almost looked like a huge spider's web on the side of a cliff.

'The great Phoenix was its first architect,' said Hcur proudly, 'and we have lived here for countless generations since, once many hundreds of us dwelt on these cliff walls. I can't recall a time when any man has stood and taken in this view, even the cats don't show themselves here often.'

'How do we reach it?' asked Austin astonished.

'A little further up there is another bridge across the canyon. Then we can climb down to it.'

'Even I admit to being amazed,' said Chajak her first words since battling their pursuer, 'and I've seen the Aerie twice before.'

'You never answered me before how many people live here Hcur?' asked Austin, excited at seeing such a place.

'There are only thirteen of us remaining, young one,' came the solemn reply.

As they made their way to the crossing, Jak spoke at last of the phantom.

'He knew, friend. Though he won't be able to tell anyone else.'

'Of the sword?' asked Hcur pulling up. 'You're sure he knew?'

'He asked me did we have it. I don't know if he had the chance to tell anyone else. That dragon maybe.' Austin didn't know what to make of this news or what it would mean.

'Dragons assassins and sorcerers, what have we let ourselves in for? We have to assume Pravus knows. But it changes nothing, after our stop at the Aerie we make straight for Aurum with even more care.'

The Great Ridge Mountains separated Ridgedale into east and west. On the west side of the great range the sides were tall and threatening almost like a stone wall reaching up to the skies. There were only three ways to get to the Capital in the east from the silver city. Go miles northeast the past the mountains which level before sea, or go even further southeast and through Ridgewood the old forest. The third was the Ridgeway. A natural channel in part but mostly it was a pass cut through the very rocks of the mountains. As the old road met the cliff walls the mountains parted slightly. It was here that the pass was made and the fortifications and gate built. Work had started on the pass generations ago and it was still not entirely complete. Various outposts and other structures some wood some stone jotted the way, an inn included, some were not ready to be used. Ten tall statues lined the route at lengthy intervals of which the four middle were again incomplete. They were the ancient Kings of Ridgedale looking down on any travellers. The path through the mountains made for an empty and eerie place; for the most part the cliff walls blocked direct sunlight onto the path, but it was wide enough to allow the old road to join the cities of Aurum and Argentum.

The Botley fortifications were complete, though. Named after the general whose idea it was to build them here, but had long since passed such was the length of time it had taken to construct them. The fortifications were almost as if a castle had been cut into the stone. They stood over and around the watch gate on the west side Ridgeway. The gateway was either called the silver gate or the golden gate depending on which way you travelled. Heading to the Argentum the gate was painted silver. On the other side it was painted gold. Maggot holes cut into the steep mountain walls above the gate allowed archers and their keen eyes to protect the pass. Troops maintained the fortifications the third largest deployment in Ridgedale after the two major cities.

A great galloping of hooves announced the arrival of Lachlan and his men. Many of the troops at on the walls cheered his coming.

'My Prince I'm Captain Bolivar we welcome you and your host to the Ridgeway,' said a soldier stepping up to great them.

'What's the latest news from the Silver City, Captain, what do our scouts report?' the colossus asked shaking the man's hand. Like all soldiers in the Ridgedale army he wore silver looking amour. On his breast plate was the design of the Golden tower. While he addressed the Prince his helmet was under his arm but when worn the front would rest on his nose with a slit to see through and the back came to the nape of his neck.'

'The news isn't good my Prince.'

'We had better prepare for the refugees of Argentum,' put in one of Lachlan's men, he was Gideon and he was the Prince's standard bearer and right hand man. Suited in golden armour but not nearly as elaborate as his Princes.

'Their already here,' added Bolivar uncomfortably as he shifted his feet.

'What where?' asked Lachlan looking around.

'We've passed very few folk on the pass where are they all now?'

'The news is grim, sir. I'm afraid to tell you that only thirty-six made it to the gate.'

'How can that be so? Many must have journeyed here,' demanded the Prince.

'They told me they were attacked en route, many fled the onslaught and may still survive but according to those who reached here most were slaughtered.

'Some hundreds were reported to have left the city. These are ill tidings indeed,' said Gideon.

'Then the Enemy is marching east already. We must make sure we're prepared for the Goblyn threat. Boomed Lachlan. 'We will make them pay dearly for this assault on our people.'

'We are as prepared as we can be, sir and welcome your troops to stand by us here,' spoke Bolivar. 'And the few scouts who have returned confirm the host of Pullus is now marching our way. But it was not the Goblyns who attacked the refugees.

'Then who was it man, speak?' demanded the Colossus. Bolivar paused as if he wasn't sure he believed the answer, or he didn't want to.

'Well, my Prince, every one of the thirty-six who arrived tell that it was a dragon who assailed them.' Gideon and Lachlan just looked at each other their faces a mixture of disbelief and fear.

Hcur led the group down into the city; they first descended a great wooden stairway that spiralled down to a platform, except for Hcur who abseiled down using an old looking but sturdy rope next to the stairs. The stairway was hidden from sight that well that Austin hadn't noticed it until they were standing over it. The stair was tucked in between a cluster of trees and near the Goodyson's edge and as it descended it led out to the canyon wall before dropping down to the Aerie. Austin thought it seemed to be made of very little and it looked precarious but it never gave an inch even with three of them on it. Then they crossed a gantry from one platform to the next until they reached what seemed to Austin as the birds' equivalent of a throne room. All the way there Braydon had at least one hand on a wall or rope and sometimes he held on with both. In the great chamber the birds gathered to welcome their visitors, all were there save for Colm who remained on sentry duty. A tall bird came forward, he had grey feathered arms and a white head, a big yellow beak and powerful yellow eyes to match.

'Welcome to the Eagles Aerie our sanctuary and our home,' he stated.

'Thank you for receiving us,' Braydon said bowing Austin nodded his agreement before bowing also.

'I am Apollo, eldest of Eagles and I speak for my people. You might say I'm leader here but we use no such term, I am no ruler or king. A Cat and two men in our nest who would have thought it would ever be so, I hope you all realise the significance of this day. A new dawn for us all perhaps?'

'We absolutely do, my Lord,' spoke Austin enthusiastically, 'and my father has been glad of your friendship.' Apollo raised his hand to stop Austin.

'I have no titles, if it pleases you to call me Lord then do so, but Apollo is fine. Let me introduce Aves and Buteo both will help you settle for your stay. Aves the Falcon shook Austin's hand first he was slighter than most other birds about Jak's size but still bigger than Austin. Like Colm his beak was grey only he had brown eyes his feathers were brown, lighter around his face getting darker as they swept away. The Buzzard known as Buteo had a yellow beak with black tip and his feathers were shades of brown with lighter specks here and there.

'Forgive me, but we bring tidings from the Silver City,' interrupted Hcur. 'Pravus attacks and his forces will soon head further east if he defeats the tower.'

'You have been travelling for a few days, old friend,' said Aves, 'and I'm afraid that is old news.'

'The sparrow flies faster than the foot marches Hcur,' added Apollo. 'The city fell three days after you left, the Dark Wizard's armies are gathering at the Ridge as we speak.' Austin's legs buckled at this news he fell to his knees. Braydon and Hcur tried to comfort him. He wanted to ask what had happened about any survivors, but he couldn't get the words out. Apollo knelt in front of him 'we know you've had a difficult journey food has been prepared you can rest here for as long as you need.' They led Austin to a table where a banquet was laid out, but he ate nothing, Braydon tucked straight in. A few birds left the chamber while they spoke.

'What brings you here?' Buteo asked Hcur. The Hawk looked at Apollo.

'Austin carries something important with him. Arian asked Chajak and I to help him deliver it to the Golden City but we felt it important you should see it first.'

'I want to say it's the gauntlets he wears. My father, also Apollo, gave them to your forefather did he not?' Austin nodded without looking up while a few of the other birds stretched to take a glance at them.

'We bring the Phoenix's sword home to the Aerie.' There were gasps from some birds, Buteo sat forward and all now looked at Austin. The great sword rested against the table near his hand still wrapped up.

'A boy now wields the Guardian's sword?' Aves said in amazement.

'Wasn't it lost a millennia ago?' asked Sek the Kestrel from the far end of the table others muttered that Hcur must be wrong the sword had been gone far too long. Apollo silenced them all.

'Friends remember the sword isn't ours it was given to men by the Firebird in a token of friendship.'

'And how did that friendship end up?' shouted Sek now standing 'they hunted us down and forced…'

'Enough,' yelled Buteo at the Kestrel. The bird looked long at them all, but sat down in a huff.

'Why did you bring the sword here Hcur?' asked Apollo. 'You must have known it would only cause division.'

'The legend concerns us also not just men.'

'And more besides,' Chajak added.

'When a new king is crowned in Ridgedale it will affect us all. We have the chance here to move forward with men and come out of hiding us and the Cats. Presenting this sword in Aurum will do that I firmly believe so.'

'But why come here?' asked Apollo again leaning back in his chair.

'We think The Dark Prince knows of it, too, and he seeks it.'

'So that's why he attacked you?' Aves suggested.

'He can't have the Guardian's sword it is bad enough he knows of it,' Braydon said in between sups from his tankard.

'Our isolation is over, if he follows you here it could mean the end of us all.' Sek spat out.

'If he reaches here the entire kingdom is already lost,' said Buteo. 'We don't have the strength to oppose Sinister you know this, Hcur, there are too few of us.'

'No, but we can take the blade to Aurum together now rather than be driven away with it. Show men that we are ready to leave the shadows and stand by them against our mutual enemy. What better way than with the sword. And united we can stand against the dark forces that would destroy us.'

'Let's not be hasty,' Apollo said, 'hasty plans often lead to failure. If you propose we abandon the Aerie then I say no.'

'Agreed,' nodded Aves, 'we can't empty the nest to help you on the quest. I respect your desire to help in this matter, Hcur, but the sword's destiny is not ours.'

'Men hid the sword many years ago didn't they? And believe in a tale about its return to save the country.' Apollo continued looking now at Austin. 'I believe in the sword, which I still don't see revealed here, but I don't hold much weight with it saving the race of men. Men are weak, present company excepted, they strike without thinking. Hcur, what is happening to man now is just a reflection of what they did to us.'

'What are you saying?' demanded Braydon.

'I would never condone Pravus and his actions but understand I'm reluctant to help save a race which nearly wiped ours out.'

'I wonder often why the firebird gave the sword to their like in the first place,' spat out Set.

'You know your history full well, as do we all,' answered Hcur. 'The sword was a gift on Luca the First's wedding day, the day Greenridge and Westerdale were united. Such an occasion deserves a fine gift and there was no greater gift than Custos Ferrum. It is not our place to judge her actions now; she was after all trying to bring our races closer.' But Sek was not about to let the matter rest so easy.

'If she knew the trouble her actions would cause …'

'Know that I would be willing to help you, Hcur,' interjected Buteo, 'but I won't oppose the wishes of Apollo wisest of us all.' A few others voiced their agreement with the Buzzard. They all pondered this for a moment. Some more drinks were sipped. Jak who had been rather quiet though all the talk suggested going to get some rest and everyone agreed, so Hcur led his three friends to a room to relax.

'You didn't say much back there, old friend?' The Hawk said to her.

'I had nothing to say, Hcur, it's not for me to decide the fate of us all, I only steer my own path.'

'There's an old saying within these walls, wise birds talk because they have something to say, foolish birds talk to hear their own voice. Perhaps keeping your own council is the smartest way of all.'

Austin could see that chaos had consumed Civitas Argentum, he could see Goblyns had surrounded his father Arian but still he fought them off, the constant clatter elsewhere let the lord of the tower know his troops were still making a stand, although he could see no friend close by. Austin could see all this through his father's eyes. Foe after foe attacked him he could not remain here his strength waned. With a mighty slash he cleaved the heads of two nearby Goblyns, a lunge at another and one more opponent fell at his feet. He decided to fall back to the tower hoping his men would do the same, they had been overrun by the numbers of the dark prince's army, and communication was now impossible. As he neared the tower he saw standing alone by the main courtyard gate a man, Arian knew instantly he wasn't one of his troops, hatred poured from this stranger, his eyes burned with it. Arian stopped maybe fifteen feet from him turned and slew some pursuing enemies, the rest stopped waiting for instruction from their master by the gate. Now face to face the two men sized each other up, after a few moments Malice drew his sword and they charged at each other. Unlike fighting the Goblyns Arian now had to contend with a warrior of considerable skill, one who seemed to be a lot fresher than himself. He took some heavy blows and delivered very few in return. Everything seem silent know. Just heavy breathing and the sound of swords clashing against each other could be heard. After what seemed like an age he fell to his knees exhausted, Malice backed off towards the courtyard gate he was saying something to his minions close by watching the duel but Arian could not make it out. He looked at his sword the image of his father and his fathers before him flashed through his mind. His family had upheld the city's liberty for five generations and he had let his them down. Shame, regret anger so many emotions poured from him. He looked up at his foe who hid his fatigue well, but why had he backed off? Austin could see that with every last bit of strength left in his body Arian hurled the Wyrm straight at the stranger. Malice had dropped his guard and barely had time to react the sword brushed his face then buried itself deep in the stone wall of the city. Malice looked at the sword then raised his own and strode toward Arian. Austin woke.

While Austin slept Braydon, Hcur and Jak discussed in the next room what they would do next. 'The Sword still needs to go to Aurum, the Birds won't help us so there's no point staying here.' Decided Braydon. 'Don't get me wrong, Hcur, this place is amazing and who else can say they've been here but it's time to go already.'

'He's right, old friend,' The Cheetah agreed. 'These are dangerous days for us all and there is no greater sin than inaction in times like these.'

'We will set out at first light then,' said Hcur. He walked over to a balcony which looked out down at the Goodyson flowing quickly past. Braydon joined him there.

'We should go now and travel fast while ...'

'No, archer, if you want to go quickly you can go now alone, but if you want to go far then we stay together and we will finish our task soon enough.'

Austin came in from his bunk with tears running down his face like rain trickling down a window.

'He's gone,' he whimpered 'I saw it in a dream as if I were there. My home has fallen to the Evil Lord.' Jak shot over to him and steered him to a chair throwing a blanket around him. 'I wish I had never left.'

'Don't think like that, your father gave you a purpose, if he has fallen the greatest honour you can do him is achieve what he asked you to do,' said the Cat.

'Your father may have escaped, lad, from what I've heard of him he was a formidable warrior,' offered Braydon.

'No I saw him fall, it was like I was actually there. And besides, father would never abandon the city, it has been razed and he has fallen.' Hcur put his feathered hand on the boy's shoulder.

'We need to carry on our journey tomorrow. I hope you have the strength to continue with us; it is becoming increasingly urgent that we get the sword to your capital.'

'I will go with you, Hcur, I have nowhere else to go.'

'If it helps Austin,' Braydon interrupted, 'I could take the sword, you can still come to Aurum with us to see your father's wish fulfilled.'

'The sword is mine.' Austin snapped. He was aware it was one of the last things his father gave him, but then realised his tone. 'I don't feel this is the right time to hand it over to anyone.'

'I'm just saying …' Braydon said hoping to change the boy's mind.

'Leave it,' Jak hissed pointing a sharp claw at the archer. 'It is his until he decides otherwise.' An uncomfortable silence fell over the group.

'How will we escape the enemy?' asked Austin after a while. 'If the Dark Forces are charging east and we now need to head back westerly won't he find us?'

'Jak has taken care of our Phantom, we know there is a Dragon in his service too, but his army won't have breached the Ridgeway yet. We will have to tread with care as always,' suggested Hcur.

'It's a shame your people won't help us I would feel safer with more friends coming with us.'

'A word of advice do not give your attention to what others will or will not do, focus it instead on what we have to do,' replied the wise Hawk. 'We have come this far and we will find a way.'

Chapter VIX: Battle of the Ridgegate

The Goblyn army had made incredible time to reach the walls of the Ridgegate. Malice had marched them hard and they were now setting up to fortifications of their own in the shadow of the mountains. He knew that the walls here would be tougher to penetrate than those of the Silver City's but he would throw everything at them none the less. While the goblin's dug their trenches and built catapults arrows rained down on them form the walls and high up in the cover of the rocks. Many where pierced and most that were succumbed to their wounds. But Malice ordered no return fire yet he just built up his strength as the hordes continued to arrive swelling his ranks beyond count.

He heard a grunt behind him and turned to see a Goblyn stooping low and gesturing to his newly erected tent. It well used and looked filthy but it kept him warm in cold nights., here was his shelter from which to direct the battle, and here he stood and surveyed his troops. He was a on a small hill not quite opposite the gate and far enough away from it to be safe from the raining arrows. It was late the sun had just set and darkness fell across the land rather appropriate thought Malice. Darkness will fall in the entire nation permanently very soon.

He took out his sword from his belt and surveyed it in the moonlight, spinning the hilt in his hand. It was slender but sturdy, the blade zigzagged three times giving it almost the look of lightning bolt. It was made of dull metal and looked dirty and used uncared for, but it was as sharp as it was deadly. Forged for him by the Goblyns it was etched with the words *'Fear and Force'* scribed in the dark language of Pullus. It's a shame he couldn't get the Wyrm out of the walls of Argentum armed with both no one would be able to oppose him.

The sound of rushing wind drew his attention and he searched the dark skies and she came into view. Venom landed near his tent her eyes and sharp white teeth all that could be seen clearly, night cloaking her form.

'So you made it at last then?' uttered Malice.

'I've been with your cousin he has chased some prey from Argentum to the forgotten lands.' The dragon hissed as she slithered closer to him.

'Who?' demanded the General.

'I don't know, but our Prince knows what the Marauder is doing.' Malice thought about this; who could be important enough for his cousin to chase? he pondered.

'He's supposed to be headed to Aurum by now,' he said finally. 'This isn't part of the plan.'

'If our Prince didn't want him to pursue he wouldn't have, plans can alter.'

'So will you be joining the battle then?' said Malice changing the subject slightly.

'When do you attack?'

'At first light I want them to see what they are up against. I want them to despair at the sight of our army, that will be my first victory.'

'You mean *our* I believe,' said Venom narrowing her eyes. Malice let out a deep breath.

'Yes of course. So will you join in the fun?'

'I will wait for my opportunity as ordered,' replied the dragon. In truth she was glad she didn't have to fight. Her only real vulnerability was numbers against her. At her size, her body was as big as a large wagon excluding her massive wingspan; she was a good target for archers and spears. That was almost her downfall many years ago and why she had hidden for in Pullus for so long. Only Pravus and his dark medicine had been able to heal her after she fell at Skull Rock. Her rock-like scales were near unbreakable but the soft flesh of her wings not nearly so. Now she would only strike smaller targets that had no chance against her, or when she had the element of surprise. Going up against an army that was prepared for them was the job of the expendable Goblyns not her. She was there to destroy the Ridgegate if she saw the opportunity.

'You may as well get comfy. We've got a ram big enough to smash the gateway,' said Malice sensing her thoughts. 'It's time to grab some sleep tomorrow will be a long day.' With that he retreated to his tent, the dragon grunted at some Goblyns close by who quickly fled away from her. She curled up to rest also.

For Malice, years of planning and battles and training where about to come to fruition. The Ridgegate was the biggest obstacle they faced, once past here sacking Aurum would be child's splay. This was the real battle where the largest concentration of enemy soldiers was to be found. When he advanced on Aurum he would have far less troops he knew there would be many casualties here, but they would have less troops also. After this no force could stop them. His armies had fought and trained in far off lands and the strongest Goblyns had become battle hardened the inexperienced would be fodder. Pravus had no real interest in those lands other than to test the strength of his forces; Malice knew they were ready and had proved so at Argentum. Nothing would stop him.

On the other side of the Ridgegate everything possible was being done to prepare for the oncoming assault. Archers crammed the ramparts so tight they barely had room to draw their bows. On the Ridgeway everyone spare was crafting arrows from anything that they could then they were taken up to the walls. The Gate was barricaded with what could be thrown against it.

'Shall we wake to see the break of a new day?' mused one soldier. Another was heard to say in a horrified tone.

'They have a dragon!' no one had seen a dragon for many a year and lived to tale the tale at least. It all added to the dismay.

The troops watched for hours in the dark light as the Goblyns massed in front of the great solid walls. Many trembled at the thought of the oncoming assault waiting for the battle to start was agony. At least when they started fighting their minds would be more occupied and the fear they felt would lessen somewhat as the need to survive kicked in. Gideon sensed this as he surveyed the rampart and yelled to all in ear shot,

'We are the King's shield we are the nation's shield never forget that.' Lachlan joined him up on the walls. 'The enemy show no fear my Prince,' he whispered then he pointed down to a Goblyn boldly leaving his trench arms held high taunting them as he stomped to the gate. He was met by a dozen arrows and fell quickly. 'This has happened a few times now,' Gideon continued. 'Sinister is telling us his forces don't fear death and he is willing to sacrifice them all to achieve his means.'

'I don't fear taunts,' boomed the Colossus so everyone could hear even his foes. With surprising agility for a man of his size wearing so much armour he leapt up on the rampart edge and pointed his sword at the dark forces'

'Rats of the evil lands,' he boomed so all could hear, 'by rights you should all be given a slow and painful death,' he paused, 'alas in my wrath my sword will strike swift and hard. Fear me as I fear no enemy.' He would taunt them now by showing them his back to address his own men he raised his sword aloft. Gideon pleaded for him to get down.

'My Captain get down their bows don't have the range of ours but with ill luck may still hit you from here.' On cue several goblin's charged closer taking aim, an arrow flew past but Lachlan didn't flinch.

'I care not,' he yelled. 'The pond scum can't even shoot straight see.' Another arrow sailed by. His own Royal guard roared their approval, joined by some of the regular army. 'Men of Ridgedale here we stand. We fight now for our freedom for our very lives. We fight for the Golden City we fight to avenge the Silver City.' He beat his free arm against his chest. 'We fight to save our families wherever in the land there are. They will strike us hard, so we will strike them harder.' His troops cheered and throwing their fists in the air. 'Who stands with me? Lachlan screamed finally. More cheers greeted this then the army started chanting his name over and over. As he went to step down an arrow struck him at last, but it only deflected off his amour and plummeted down the face of the walls. He laughed as did all around him. It was a sign he thought, there was no doubt in the mind of the Colossus who would win this battle.

Leland had lost all his strength, even if the hour wasn't so late he would still be in his bed. His once strong hands now were brittle and would shake if he lifted them so he gave up and let them lie on his sheets. The king's once keen blue eyes seemed lost, unfocused and grey. He took loud deep breaths but they were slow and weren't regular. Leuan was sleeping in a chair next to his father's bed. Leland wanted to speak to him but the words would not leave his mouth. He closed his eyes in frustration and a tear rolled down his cheek. Then another.

Leuan stirred and sat up.

'Father are you OK?' he asked reaching for the king's hand. Leland managed a feeble nod. He had so much to say to his son but could now remember none of it and none of what he did recall seemed important.

'I want you to know that I will do everything I can to make things right with my brother.' The Constant smiled he knew his son was lying but didn't have the will to do anything else. He just hoped beyond hope that maybe his son was telling the truth for once. Then he wished for a bit of Lachlan's boundless strength right now is the wrong time to give up, he thought, there's too much going on. Would he see his firstborn again? Had he sent his son to his death? Deep down he knew the forces of Pravus were overwhelming that is why he ignored the threat it just seemed too big to deal with. Too big to comprehend even. Now both his sons would face that danger he hid from and Lachlan would face it very soon indeed.

'He'll be alright, Father; he has your strength and will.' Leland thought of this for a moment then managed to give Leuan's hand a small squeeze. Is that why his body had given up? Had all his will, all his might gone to the Ridgeway with his son?

'Forgive the intrusion General but it will be light soon,' said the Goblyn Lieutenant in his raspy tones, Malice slowly sat up and dismissed him with his hand. He rubbed his face and looked at his armour heaped on the floor. Soon it would be time. The light of dawn would fall across the Ridgeway for the last time, in hours it would be rubble. He donned his skeletal looking armour slowly then left his tent and another Goblyn passed him a plate of food and a tankard.

'Any change?' he asked his minion.

'Nothing,' the Goblyn answered, 'our forces are ready for your orders.'

'Then we proceed as I've set out. Make sure they're ready.' The Goblyn slunk away and barked at others as they left. Slowly the catapults were drawn into position, fifteen of them ready to fire at first light. A Goblyn Brute near the tent started banging a big drum, feet stamped and weapons clashed on shields in time with it. Dum dum dum dum was the slow beat, and it continued long into the battle. The sound of the drums echoed off the steep walls of the Ridgeway many men there couldn't help but cover their ears.

Light slowly crept over the Ridgeway and the soldiers on those walls finally saw the extent the numbers they faced. The whole valley leading up the gate was swarming with the enemy as far as could be seen. Things had looked bad the night before but now it seemed worse still. They still had a few hopes though, firstly the Ridgegate had never been breached before, granted an army this size had never attacked it. Secondly they had The Colossus.

On Malice's order the catapults fired simultaneously and great rocks were propelled into the defences. A host of Goblyn's swarmed towards the foot of the walls and started lighting fires especially by the gateway. The Darksiders archers fired at the men on the walls who fired back with better accuracy. The catapults continued hurling rocks and more even, quite often the Goblyn's loaded them with their own fallen comrades. They made little impact on the walls but could cause damage if hitting by chance a soldier upon them. This struck more fear into the Royal army if they could do that to their own how far were they willing to go?

An hour went by and the Ridgegate was now littered with the fallen but there seemed no end to their number. Arrows still rained down from the maggot holes and the fortifications but they were now running out. Archers cried out for more many soldiers resulted in throwing anything they could while they waited for some. While the Goblyn numbers had been hit the men they faced had taken serious loses too. The enemies aim wasn't great but the sheer weight of numbers they threw at the walls took its toll. Fires blazed below but the Gate held firm.

By the second hour the pace of the fighting had slowed down. The Dark Prince's troops were hampered by their own dead in their way, and all the arrows were spent on the walls. Efforts were redoubled to craft more and salvage what they could. Fires still raged but the gate wouldn't light, still it held firm. The Goblyns cleared a path to the gate pushing their dead aside and a great battering ram drew up to it. Lachlan's soldiers dropped flaming liquid over it having no arrows to fire at the foes who dragged it. No matter how many were burnt the Goblyns still dragged it closer and soon it was hammering the Gateway, again their numbers were prevailing.

Venom now saw her chance without arrows flying at her she happily rushed at the Ridgegate. She strafed the walls and ramparts flames missing those who were lucky dive for cover but killing many including Bolivar and many of his best men. She did this a few times and soon the ramparts where bare, and the smoke billowed from the maggot holes. She landed by the battering ram stood on her rear legs and let out a great breath. An inferno spewed from inside her assailing the great wooden doorway that creaked and burnt and finally gave up its own fight. The dragon smiled and took to the air while the hordes swarmed in. Malice ordered the catapults move in closer so they now pounded the great fortifications which offered no opposition, but he was taking no chances he would still knock them to the ground.

The Colossus tried to rally his troops and he led them now head on to greet the oncoming mass. This was his type of fight at last; close combat no more shooting from distance. He had hated watching the battle take place in front of him while he stood idly by; now his thick sword held high he charged his foes. He fought like a man possessed. His Golden Flame, as his sword was known, danced through the air destroying anything it made contact with. Goblyns swarmed around him attacking with swords of their own, spears and clubs even, but to no avail. Some even tried to tackle him with rope to slow him down, but the Colossus raged. Goblyn bodies most without all their limbs littered the ground around him. At one point he plunged his blade so far into the chest of one foe that when he fell it took the weapon with him. The Darksiders thought this was their chance to take him down, but they were wrong as now he used their weapons instead and rocks and his own fists were also enough. He grabbed the ankle of one of his foul opponents and swung him at two more nearing him before freeing his own blade once again.

His own men were both in awe at this mighty warrior a prince who no man or beast could oppose. He gave them hope, inspiring them to fight on. A would be king fighting with ordinary men like them. But at the same time those near him were shocked at the madness in his eyes. At the ruthlessness that now possessed him. Lachaln didn't need to venture far to find a foe, Goblyns kept coming to him over and over soon the ground under his feet was soaked black with their blood.

Malice decided it was time. He ordered for his shield and eleven of his troops formed a barrier around him as he marched, they were identified by their blood red armour. If one Goblyn was shot down or stabbed another quickly replaced him in the ranks. In this way Malice was able to reach the Colossus. His shield parted and the hordes attacking Lachlan stopped: The Prince against a man who could have been one. They fought hard. Malice was a battle hardened warrior stronger than most but Lachlan was sheer strength and self-belief. Neither were young men, both had total self-belief. Their swords clashed at first the blows were quick both seeking the advantage but after a while the blows slowed down tiring under each other's pressure. After some five minutes of intense striking, but what seemed much longer to both, the Colossus started to gain the upper hand.

His blows still rained hard on Malice whose strength faltered it became all he could do to parry them. Lachlan's confidence became such that he could now even pick off one or two Goblyn's who stood too close by the action and weren't paying attention.

It seemed the tide had turned in favour of the Royal Army the Goblyn's including Malice's shield could no longer afford the time to watch the two behemoths battle they were being forced back. Gideon and others inspired by Lachlan's feats pushed back against the enemy force. With a stiff boot to Malice's midriff and an almighty swing of his huge sword the dark lord's general finally fell to his knees. The Colossus stood tall over Malice sword in both hands above his head ready to bring down on his foe. He never got the chance to though.

Venom watching, circling the battle high above, had seen the whole skirmish with her keen eyes, now as she wasn't the focus she dived down at frightening speed and grabbed at Lachlan. She caught hold of his sword with one talon and an arm with another. She carried him high up and flung him with fury against the solid walls of the Ridgeway. The Colossus smashed into the stone and rolled and fell back down the rocky wall. Many of his bones were already broken when he landed hard on a small ledge which saved his life momentarily, a plummet to the foot of the walls would have been certain death. Slowly he scrambled up to one knee using his only working hand to lean on the wall. Regaining his senses he caught sight of the dragon, he cursed her defiantly. Venom circled back round to the Prince and met him with an enormous jet of flame. Fire bounced back of the rocks such was its intensity the heat cracked the stone and the ledge fell. No remains of Lachlan would be found, the heir to Ridgedale was incinerated in that moment.

Archers now had more ammunition at last but it was too late, Venom was forced away by arrows shot at her by the despairing men below, she fled from their range smiling at the significance of her actions. Fear quickly took hold of the Royal Army, the gate was breached the Botley fortifications destroyed and now their hero had fallen. It was Gideon the last ranking soldier to be found who finally gave the order to retreat not long after the Prince's death. Most had turned and run anyway, such was the importance of the Colossus.

The Golden City was quiet that day; when Lachlan publicly rode off to the Ridgeway a few days before it got folk talking as yet no news had been heard. Normally everyone knew what the Prince was up to, and all enjoyed stories about him. The people of Aurum loved their king and loved his sons, too, being as brash as he was somehow made Lachlan more endearing to them. Whispers now spread like wildfire over dry bush about the king's health. The king was an important figure in all their lives, while few ordinary folk had met him even less had seen him recently, but he had always been there. It was inevitable most said, we all must pass on, and the king had lived so very long. But all were saddened by the thought of losing him. The eldest of them fondly told tales of the king as a young man rebuilding the city after the abuse it suffered under the tyrant Kraig. And he helped out literally carrying bricks with his soldiers for the best bricklayers and masons he could find to craft new walls. It didn't matter that he had been king for a few years already he still mucked in and helped out. He would be mourned in the Golden city without a doubt.

Leuan remained by his father's side as he had for the last few hours. The king's breath was painfully slow and Leuan often sat up thinking it had stopped praying for another breath which ultimately came. This went on for hours. While the king slept many came to see him and pay respects, all now knew it was only a matter of time. Counsellor's important citizens Lords and Knights, physicians the Conniving let them come but only a short time each, physicians aside. He had given up talking to his father, instead he let him rest. At this moment he had no thoughts of thrones in his mind, no schemes were being plotted, he just sat and comforted his king no his father if he could. He thought for a short while of what was happening west at the Ridgegate he too was concerned by the lack of news from there, he put these thoughts and those of his brother to the back of his mind for now though. Then tears rolled down his cheeks and he sobbed uncontrollably for several minutes. As much as he wanted the crown he didn't want to give up his father he realised.

So it was that as Lachlan perished on the walls of the Ridgeway his father back home in his Golden Tower also took his last breath.

Chapter X: A Lion King

Austin and his friends slept well that night knowing they were safe in the Eagles Aerie. When he awoke Austin looked over the ravine and wondered how many people had stood in this spot and contemplated their futures. He knew Hcur well now and understood how wise and learned his was, and the other birds he had met seemed cut from similar cloth. Quite a few must have stood here with their heads full of thoughts he decided.

'How are you this morning, lad?' Austin turned to see his wise friend approach him.

'I can't put the images of my father battling in the streets of home out of my head. I'm never going to see him again am I?'

'I can't answer that for certain. But until it's known otherwise never forget there is a chance he's alive.' Austin looked down and gave his head a little shake.'

'Who will we give the sword to in Aurum, Hcur?' he said at last.

'Another question I can't answer wholly,' answered the bird. 'I had thought we would present it to the council or the princes.'

'I had the same idea, but how will we bring it to them and would they see us?' Austin looked around and lowered his voice. 'And what of Braydon I like him and he wants the sword?'

'He is a variable your father never foresaw for us on the road isn't he? He is strong and courageous he has the spirit of a warrior with the heart of a leader. The legend of the sword could easily be interpreted so that a man such as him could take the crown.'

'I think he would be a good king it seems to me he knows more of life in Ridgedale than of anyone in the golden city. Maybe because he's not from there.'

'Perhaps you're right, lad. The sword was entrusted to you and I can't make the decision for you. But I will do anything I can to help you and remember no decision has to be made here.'

'You always seem to know what to say and have advice Hcur I'm glad to have your companionship on the road the journey would have been almost impossible without you.'

'Nonsense you're a clever lad you would have found a way I'm merely here to assist you. As for me being wise well I've lived a long time by your reckoning and I'm constantly learning. I've made plenty of mistakes in my youth the trick is to learn from them remember Austin, if you are not willing to learn no one can ever help you. A word of advice if you are determined to learn no one will ever stop you. I won't stand here and tell you what to do or order you to do this or that, but I will always keep telling you to have an open mind and always be ready to learn.' Austin nodded, Hcur put his hand on his shoulder, 'The setbacks we have faced to get here with the sword we have somehow dealt with, if we get knocked down five times we get up six.'

'Rise, fall down, rise again, that was something my father said.'

'Then it's good advice and it reminds me of the Phoenix ever reborn, I'll have to remember that one.' The hawk looked past Austin and saw Braydon and Jak joining them they both looked anxious.

'What's wrong, friends?' he asked.

'It seems our departure will be delayed,' replied Jak.

'Why?' asked Austin.

'My people are coming and they want to see us,' answered the cheetah.

They now gathered in the same hall they ate and talked in the previous day. All set to continue their journey. Isis the Kite and the finest tailor amongst the birds had worked all night to patch any holes in their garments and provide Braydon with something more suitable than his stolen gear. He now wore navy slacks which went under his high dark green boots and he had a green tunic and jacket. The jacket looked bulky but was finely embroidered an image of an eagle in flight on its back. Apollo also provided Braydon with a bow and a quiver stuffed with arrows for which he was very grateful, along with a suitable sheath for the Sword of the Moon. Austin no longer had the Guardians sword wrapped up it now hung in a newly crafted scabbard from beautiful leather belt again provided by their hosts.

'Do we have to wait for them, can't we leave now?' asked Austin.

'They know you're here and it isn't wise to cross a lion,' spoke Apollo.

'Why are they coming?' Braydon asked Hcur, but Apollo answered.

'They come because I told them the sword was due to arrive here, I had expected them sooner.' He looked now at the Hawk. 'You did say the Guardian's sword will affect us all, we believed they had the right to know.'

'I have no problem with Magnus and his cats knowing of our mission only with the delay.'

'It can't be helped brother and you know his temper. Once he has said whatever it is he has to say you can 'continue,' Apollo went to turn away before adding, 'he may offer you aid, the scouts tell us a great number are on route.'

'That isn't what my instincts are telling me.'

'He has the same right to know of our quest as Apollo. And it would be a great help if my king would assist us,' added Jak hopefully 'any more pursuers would think twice before challenging with a pride of cats at our back.'

Hcur tried smiling at his companion 'We shall see my friend.'

'He's a king?' interrupted Austin 'but Leland…'

'Magnus is the king of all cats, boy. Said Jak, 'before the arrival of men the cats ruled all these lands.

The lion Magnus who was the known as the king of cats and he carried himself as such, he was big, Austin thought, assuming he would be look a little like Chajak. Instead he was much broader with powerful arms none of the cats wore sleeves he had noticed. Magnus's large eyes and their deep black pupils pierced him. Three others entered with him a tiger and two panthers whose fur was charcoal black. Magnus wore blue like most of the cats only his was much richer and his great mane burst from his wide collar and flowed down his back. His tail flicked as he walked. When he spoke he flashed his yellow white teeth menacingly.

'Greetings Apollo, greetings Chajak so the sword of the Phoenix has returned has it? He growled in his deep voice. 'Who do we have here?' Apollo introduced Hcur who then introduced the others.

'This is Braydon an Archer of Ridgedale,' the other big cats muttered to themselves at this, 'and may I present the sword's current Guardian, Austin, son of Arian, captain of the silver city.' The lion shook Austin's hand with his huge paw-like one.'

'Your grace,' Austin bowed as did Braydon.

'Allow me to introduce my second in command Jett' The Tiger standing to Magnus's right stepped forward. He was taller than the lion but not so broad, a look of hatred of which he did nothing to hide poured from him. He didn't extend his hand to greet the others.

'So the fate of these lands lies in your small hands?' he spat out, then he turned to Jak, 'and you travelling with that.' He nodded at Braydon, Jak seemed to shrink though she tried to look defiant. Magnus raised his hand to stop Jett from going on. Austin could now see all the cats were armed even the king. The hilts of their swords could be seen over each of their left shoulders.

'You look fit and well, soldier of Ridgedale, so can I presume you've never seen our like before meeting Chajak?' asked the King.

'I have not your grace,' Braydon answered truthfully 'though I have heard of your people in old tales.'

'I thought as much. It has been known for men to come from Aurum from time to time in an attempt to hunt us. As such your race isn't very popular in these parts. But as you're here and breathing I presume you've never done so after all only a handful of men have ever left our lands to see another day. The Crown Prince of yours is one.' Austin and Braydon looked at each other unsure what to say or do.

'I'll get right to the point,' continued Magnus, 'that sword you carry will create a new kingdom over these lands.' He crossed his arms. 'And I want both.'

'Over my dead body!' shouted Braydon pushing Austin behind him while reaching for his own blade. Quick as a flash Jett and several other cats had theirs drawn also and were roaring. Chajak had also unsheathed her own swords. Magnus just refolded his arms across his broad chest. Apollo raised both his hands to calm the cats, Hcur tried to likewise with Braydon.

'Were all friends here there is no need for arms?' Apollo said loudly. 'Magnus I have allowed their expedition to continue and they have my blessing to leave, though not my support. However I cannot allow you to take the sword from them by force. Not here.'

'This is your den and I won't jeopardise our age old alliance here. This matter will not be dropped though.' Magnus offered before turning to Jak. 'You side against your own?' The cheetah lowered her weapons.

'I have travelled with Hcur many times as you know, my king, he has earned my complete trust and respect. He and I vowed to the boy's father to see the sword taken to Aurum.

'And to fulfil your vow you would oppose you own kind?'

'I did not in my wildest dreams imagine that I would have too.' The cat paused. 'But I will not break my word.'

'Perhaps I was wrong to send you to them. Maybe no contact at all with the race of men would be best from now on.'

'What's happened is in the past, we now know of the sword because of our emissaries. Apollo interjected. 'If you want the blade it might be wise to go to the golden city with them and make your claim when it is revealed.'

'No,' interrupted Magnus 'this is what will happen. One of two things will decide if the Guardian's sword leaves here in my hand or yours, boy. Firstly I challenge you to it right here man to man. Or secondly I will seize it when you leave the city. I have more than enough cats eyes out there to keep a sharp watch on the Aerie for a long long time.'

'Magnus?' questioned Apollo he was disturbed by the attitude of the lion, he unlike the others knew what the great cat was truly like. The power of Custos Ferrum has him under its spell he realised. The Guardian's sword tempted all with its promise of power. But Apollo also knew it was unwise to argue with the lion who was used to getting his own way.

'I said I won't take it by force in your home and I'm a Lion of my word. But outside of the Aerie the rules are different. Decide your fate, boy,' snarled the big cat.

'He is no match for you king of lions,' said Hcur, 'you will destroy him for the weapon?'

'Absolutely we will do what it takes to put ourselves on terms with his kind.' Roared Jett.

'What Jett means is that for too long have we hidden away on our little island. With the sword in my possession we could come out of the shadows and be free from the threat of persecution. If,' Magnus shook his head 'no when we have the sword men will accept us as equals no longer will we be forced to stay on our little rock. Centuries ago men pushed us from our rightful lands, when I have the sword we will no longer hide. It will mean you will be free, too, Apollo,' His voice was always loud and there was no mistaking its menacing tone.

'I won't give you it you will have to take it from me' uttered Austin trying to sound like he wasn't frightened of the lion. He did his best to hide the fact he was shaking.

'This, Apollo, is why I won't go to Aurum; the boy's mind is already set against me, the sword of the great Phoenix, your ancestor, is destined to remain with men in his mind.'

Silos and his slender-hooded companion made their way to Leuan's chamber, it had been a day since the king's passing and the prince had hidden away all that time. Knocking on the wooden door they were permitted entry and slowly entered the room. It was dark; drapes covered all the windows though some light crept in past the sides. Silos offered his condolences once more as he sat at a table in the centre of the room he could just make out Leuan in the shadows.

'Take a seat, councillor, I hope you bring good news.' He looked at the companion. 'Remove that hood before your prince.' He wasn't expecting to see a woman under the hood, she was tall and thin with short hair and dark eyes, much like his own she had eyes that many plots and secrets lay behind.

'You bring a girl before me, Silos, is she to cheer me up?' he quipped.

All women have their uses your highness from big to small. They have ruled us in the distant past. Imagine that – a Queen to rule us, I have no problem with the idea of a queen, but she should be sat by her king's side looking resplendent don't you think?' Silos ignored his companion's stern glare. 'Don't misunderstand me, women have their uses and many and important roles at that. But to rule? I think not. But allow me to introduce Catalina my intelligencer. My top agent if you will. All the plots and counterplots around the kingdom, all the whispered words in the night and knives in the dark are hers to unravel and decipher, and she does her job very well. That I've not been assassinated several times by men after my position is entirety down to her and her agents.' Leuan looked impressed and nodded to her to join them at the table.

'You do play an important role don't you; I can understand why others want your position. So what can tell me this grey afternoon?'

'Firstly, my prince, there is still no news from the mountains…'

'You need an intelligencer to tell me that?' scoffed Leuan. 'I can tell you that already!'

'Please, my prince, allow me to finish. Looking at the greater scheme of things we have to assume that the forces at the Ridgegate are unable to send word to us. This means they are most likely defeated or close to it.'

'I had thought the same things,' said Leuan shaking his head.

'What this means is you could be King, sir.'

'You think I don't realise that?' Spat the prince now exasperated. 'Your endless fountain of knowledge inspires me.' The three sat in silence for a few moments, Leuan carefully looking over Catalina like a hyena looking at its prey. 'Tell me more of yourself intelligencer, how does a girl become as informed as you in a kingdom such as this?'

'I will not reveal my secrets, my prince, I hope you can appreciate the delicate nature of my business.' She had a soft voice but it had a hard edge to it. The dark spark remained in her eyes. She wore dark greens and black, her age was impossible to guess.

'You refuse a direct request from me?' He liked her already.

'And I beg your forgiveness for doing so,' she answered sternly. Yes there was a connection and they both knew it.

'As the eyes of the council leader do you ever get your hands dirty?' he asked next. She looked at him suspiciously, as did Silos.

'My hands will never again be clean, for the longer I wash up the more muck I have to deal with.'

'I don't know where you're going with this, my prince,' Silos added, she didn't answer.

'Are you wealthy, intelligencer?'

'Very, in knowledge, not nearly so in coin.'

'A certain councillor knows too many of my true thoughts, change is needed in I feel.' Leuan continued as Silos trembled. 'If I were to offer a promotion of sorts how far would you go to take it?'

'Sir I must…' Silos never finished his sentence, Catalina had cut his throat with an elegant knife that dropped from her sleeve, and he slumped forward onto the table.

'Is that far enough?' she asked Leuan.

'Well you are ruthless aren't you? ` He said with a smile. They both knew they didn't need Silos now they had been introduced to each other. He would just be a complication. Leuan had planned to have him murdered soon anyway, he was delighted with his new agent.

'Let's go somewhere more private I have plans.'

'Well then keeper of the sword, do you accept my terms? I grow weary of waiting for your answer,' demanded Magnus. Austin gripped the sword close, he could see no escape. He was glad his friends, his only friends really, were close, without them he would have lost the sword long ago. Now that seemed inevitable.

It was Braydon who answered though.

'I accept on his behalf as I claim the blade, too, and it would be a fairer duel.' He turned to Austin, 'I still don't ask for it now or even if I prevail, only when you are ready.' Magnus thought about this for a moment.

'Any objections Apollo, Hcur?' asked the Lion. They could think of none though neither could see another way out of the situation. 'Then prepare yourself soldier of men.' Magnus unsheathed his own sword it was another fine blade Austin seemed to have seen many recently. Like the Guardian's sword it was mostly silver. It had a red gem at the bottom of its hilt, its handle was a twisting column leading to red and silver wings before its long blade began. There was also a likeness an eagle on the hilt in between the wings. Hcur whispered to Austin

'That is also a blade of the Phoenix and a very great sword indeed. Magnus's sword is the Defender's sword. Some say it is the sister to yours.'

Magnus raised it over his head the tip pointed at Braydon. The archer stepped forward a few paces then raised the long sword he had found in the bandit's wagon. They fought. Sword on sword steel on steel echoed around the great hall. Magnus was stronger and more skilled with the blade and slowly wore Braydon down. If it were a competition with a bow few would best him, but Braydon's skill was not with the blade. A kick to Braydon's gut knocked the wind out of him, soon Magnus disarmed his foe and sent him sprawling across the floor. With his foe's sword out of reach the Lion turned his back on his foe to address the others.

'This is your champion? Your would-be king?' he mocked, 'Your great protector?' Austin behind the Lion's back without thinking tossed the Guardian's sword to Braydon. It landed near him and he grabbed it as Magnus spun round its tip was at the lion's throat before he knew it.

'Yield!' Braydon demanded.

'I will never kneel before a man.' Braydon pressed the weapon into the lions golden mane, Magnus's eyes narrowed. They stared at each other for what seemed to all watching as an eternity. Jett drew his own blade but Braydon didn't flinch totally focused on his opponent. The king of lions flicked his wrist signalling the Tiger to stand down. Finally Magnus released his sword and it dropped to the floor.

'I underestimated you; I concede the duel but not my claim on the sword. Not yet, *man*,' he sneered slowly.

Braydon lowered the Guardian's sword and he marvelled at it once more. It had won the fight without striking a blow or even being swung in anger at another. Magnus picked up his sword and roared at his fellows then he left quickly.

Braydon passed the sword back to Austin, he wanted to take it back but stuttered.

'It's yours now you have triumphed with it in battle.' He knelt before Braydon, Hcur and Jak looked at each other and then bowed at Braydon too.

'So it's decided then,' said Hcur.

'Thank you for your faith in me, Austin, but for now will you carry the Phoenix sword like you have so well through so many perilous days? On the gates of Aurum I will take it back where all can see.'

Austin was confused and could only say, 'If you wish.' Though he was relieved to be keeping the sword for a bit longer.

'Then think of yourself as my squire then or something like that,' he laughed as he ruffled Austin's hair.

Chapter XI: To the Golden City

Jett and the panthers with him made a lot of fuss before leaving with their king, none seemed to think the matter was settled yet. And in truth all knew nothing was settled yet. Jett even attempted to challenge Braydon before finally following Magnus. It was late now and Hcur's plan of leaving early that morning was in tatters, the cats now surrounded the Aerie while all thought of what to do next. Austin sat in Hcur's room with his friends no words had been spoken for some time.

After a while Apollo entered with Aves and Buteo in tow.

'What do you plan to do next, Hcur?' the eagle asked.

'We can't stay here' that much is certain but we can't leave without Magnus knowing,' answered the hawk. 'He will pursue us.'

'You can understand why he wants the blade?'

'That doesn't mean we give it to him.'

'I've never seen you like this old friend. You're determined like never before,' said Apollo crossing to near the Balcony. He looked down at the flowing Goodyson. 'You can leave by boat they might not expect that.'

Hcur stood and thought about this all the others looked up. Apollo continued 'they line all the banks above us and would certainly see you at some point but you should get a good head start.'

'Agreed,' nodded Hcur, Austin stood up by him.

'What if they catch us?' he asked.

'We won't let them, gather your stuff, friends, were leaving.' Jak gave a big grin and Braydon shrugged his agreement.

Soon they were descending to the lower levels of the city, the birds wrapped them in large black cloaks in order to hide them from the eyes of the cats. They reached a platform at the bottom of the Aerie and could go no further. Braydon looked over the side a few small wooden boats were tied up on a bank still at least forty feet below them. He looked around as did Jak and Austin.

'How do we get down?' he asked the Hawk quietly in case anyone was watching.

'There should be a rope ladder here,' replied the hawk searching for it.

'There's nothing here,' said Jak. Austin took out his rope.

'What about this,' he suggested.

'Good lad,' said Hcur Braydon gave him a playful dig in the arm as Jak tied it to the side of the platform. As soon as it was tight she leapt over the side and lowered herself to the bottom in a matter of seconds she was there. Braydon was next he took a little longer but was also soon down. He held the rope as Jak untied a boat. Austin went next and scrambled down, his hands were raw when he finished and he took a deep breath in relief. When Hcur was almost down the rope came free and the bird fell the last few feet, hitting the bank he fell a few steps and splashed his ankles into the river. All immediately looked up and around to see his anyone had seen or heard them.

'I thought you tied the rope!' he whispered to Jak. An exasperated look across his face.

'I did!' Austin knew the rope would come free, just as it had over the Sovereign and for his father. He gave a smile as they all got into the boat. They discussed taking two but decided one would less likely be seen and they could all stay together even if it would be more cramped. They all got in and Jak pushed them away and jumped in the rear as Braydon and Hcur paddled. Austin sat at the front watching the way ahead the rest had eyes up looking for the cats. It wasn't long before they heard a great roar from above them.

Reon the Puma saw them first from high up on the cliff, he raised the alarm roaring to his fellows, but was immediately in a conundrum. They were to be taken alive but how could they be stopped down there? He could shoot them with his bow but that might injure them or worse sink the boat and take the sword with it. He decided to follow it as best he could, though it was hard to track it far down below in the dark of night.

When Jett heard the roars he went quickly to find out what they were, upon learning of the fleeing boat he charged right back to Magnus who stayed at the top of the stairs to the city. On his return though Apollo was there with nine of his kin.

Shortly before offering Hcur and company a way to leave via the canyon the great birds all met to discuss the events that had unfolded. Opinion was split on what action to take if any. Some counselled inaction others wanted to help Hcur, a minority thought about aiding the cats. Ultimately all would follow without question any decision made by Apollo such was his standing with the bird folk. He listened to all arguments and arrived at the conclusion that he couldn't help Magnus, he was troubled that the lion king threw his weight around in the Aerie. He knew the big cat as well as any and knew that was not his typical behaviour he had always shown nothing but respect in the Aerie before. The Guardian's sword temptation was too great for him, and if he actually held it what would he be like then? Would their friendship continue as it was? No he had to get the weapon away from Magnus and that meant aiding Hcur which he had been reluctant to do. Now he had no choice. His plan was twofold: first get the sword out of the city by river as it would be harder to chase; the cats were all up high on the canyon walls. Secondly bait the lion.

'My king they flee with the sword as we knew they would, the cowards,' growled Jett. 'They've a boat, Reon follows them.'

'So it seems, Apollo here has just told me,' snarled Magnus. 'We will catch them. I feel let down by you old friend.' Apollo only sighed and shook his head.

'You shouldn't have come to our nest and thrown your orders around,' Apollo said at last. 'I see now that it would best for all if the sword was far away from here and from you.' He calmly stated as he took a staff from behind his back. The Eagle now wore silver looking gauntlets and a red cloak flowed down his back from shoulders, steel greaves covered his shins and knees. The other birds where similarly armoured.

'What?' Magnus raged, but the Eagle continued.

'You've dishonoured my home my guests and my kin with your actions here. I've a greater claim to Custos Ferrum than you, but my honour and word mean more to me.'

Aves brought out a ball and chain and slowly it started to spin, Buteo now gripped and battle-axe in both hands, the other birds had produced weapons of their own. The cats all yelled at the air except Magnus whose eyes never left Apollo's. Slowly he reached over his shoulder for his sword; the other cats did the same. Apollo didn't move.

'It would have been so much wiser to turn the firebird's blade over to us.' Magnus spoke. 'It would have spared you pain.'

'The Phoenix taught us to do what is right not what is easy,' Apollo answered unflinching.

'Then she was wrong!' boomed the lion and with that he charged. Without missing a beat the other cats did likewise. Tigers Panthers Leopards Jaguars Cheetahs and more all sprang forward. The birds were outnumbered.

Two days after the king's death two riders reached the Civitas Aurum swift as their horses could run. The first arrived a full hour before the second a runner from the Royal army. Both riders raced from the Ridgeway neither knew of each other. The first rider had no uniform and would have been largely ignored by the city's citizens if he hadn't been travelling at break neck speed though the streets. He reached his rendezvous point a small stone house near the main gate, it was almost invisible tucked in-between other larger houses. He turned a key in the lock and shoved the thick door wide, as he expected no one was there it was not a scheduled meeting time. But he knew what to do in times like these, the building was mostly bare no windows only a table and a two chairs in the only room. There was a fire though, and wood to light it. The rider quickly had one going and smoke rose through the chimney that squeezed its way between the other buildings. Now he had to wait for the only other person in Ridgedale who had a key to that door, he prayed she arrived soon.

Catalina took twenty minutes to arrive and receive news that the Ridgeway had fallen. She immediately took that news to the Leuan.

The conniving was in the great hall with the council many things were being discussed, the whereabouts of Silos was a pressing issue no one had seen him for a day. Leuan had ordered publicly he be summoned right away. Some speculated he was in grieving for the king. The succession was another issue being discussed, but no word from the walls about Lachlan delayed any plans from going ahead. The Prince refused to send out any more riders or scouts to the Ridgeway, too many had gone and none returned so far. He would wait till word reached back before taking a course of action, and though he was second in line to the throne he was in command in the Crown prince's absence so his order was obeyed.

Catalina received many stares as she entered the hall and approached Leuan. He sat in his chair next to his father's grand throne, she approached bowed and whispered in his ears. The conniving face showed no emotion; in fact he froze lost in his own world for many moments. It was only the arrival of the second rider at the hall's great doors that brought him back. The runner from the army sprinted into the hall and announced to all that the Ridgegate had been breached and that the host of Pullus was now unopposed. This was a shock to the council panic spread throughout the chamber, to Leuan this was confirmation of what Catalina had told him. An older councillor shouted at the rider about news of Lachlan. The rider shook his head fell to his knees tears in his eyes. Leuan suppressed a smile while Catalina settled into a chair next to him. He was now king.

The clash lasted far longer than Magnus would have liked but ultimately he was victorious. The birds fought valiantly but in the end couldn't cope with the aggression and most tellingly the numbers of the cats. The cats were mighty warriors on their own but three on one the birds, fine warriors also, stood no chance. Magnus recognised bravery, though, however misguided he believed it may be. And while the birds were hurt and some badly all their lives were spared. His anger still needed some satisfaction though, therefore he ordered that Eagles Aerie be burned, a task the always hot-headed Jett jumped at. That would be fitting for Apollo's treachery the lion king thought and it would hurt the eagle a great deal. Attention now went to chasing the boy and the sword.

All resistance was squashed and as in Civitas Argentum no prisoners were left by Malice's orders. Those men who couldn't flee to the golden city were mostly the wounded and they were soon slaughtered. The General of the Goblyn army had sent three hundred of his troops after the fleeing men; he had no hopes of them taking the city they were just the first wave, the announcement of what was to come. He gathered all his forces together he afforded them a rest, they had earned it he grudgingly conceded. Tomorrow they would march on.

Venom had earlier arrived back at the dark city of Acerbus to tell Pravus personally of their success. The black Prince was indeed pleased. He clenched his gauntlets in delight and let out a sickening laugh. Like Malice he knew the resistance at the capital would not compare with that of the great walls. Soon Ridgedale would be his. Sinister prepared to leave he wanted to be there to see that city fall, after all he had waited for this moment for so long. Should he go with Venom he thought, and be seen riding the magnificent Dragon into the last battle that would be an image never forgotten? Or should he simply cast a spell, he'd arrive quicker and it would be a reminder to all, as if they needed it, how powerful a sorcerer he was. One issue remained though, he turned back to Venom his oldest servant.

'Go back and find Marauder. He should be returning now hurry him along I want him at Aurum with us.'

'As you command oh great lord,' answered Venom and with that she hauled herself to a window and took off into the sky. I liked the idea of arriving on Dragon back he thought but some things were more important.

Pravus glided to his cauldron and waved his hands over it. He had to cover all bases now he needed to know what was going on and be kept up to date. He waved his hands over the black pot chanting dark words, till finally he raised his hands towards the roof of his cavern as a gust of steam gushed up. The steam cloud slowly turned into a swarm of black moths which darted around the room. Pravus knew what was happening with Malice he had led the dark forces well. But the general's cousin where was he? He needed answers.

'Follow Venom, report back anything no matter how trivial. Go!' With that the cloud of moths flew of after Venom.

'Gentlemen you must have heard the news. We are on the back foot the enemy is on the move.' Leuan stood in front of his father's throne as he addressed the great hall, anyone of importance in Aurum and those who just thought they were there also. The council was there of course, along with the Knights who led the army including the city's guard, and wealthy men of the city. The conniving summoned them all. 'Swift action is now needed no longer can we wait and see what the dark lord will do. Strong leadership is required and quickly. I propose to push forward my coronation as soon as possible; the populace needs to see us take decisive action.' He looked out at the faces all were on him, he could see grief in most of them terror in many.

Catalina slipped into the chamber and stood in the corner of the hall unnoticed by most of them no one knew her purpose there after all. No other sources of hers from the west had reported to her since the news from the gateway. Usually this wouldn't be too big an issue to her, agents often went weeks without contact. But only when there was nothing to report. There must be so many issues to bring to her ears right now so what was the delay? The most likely reason was they were unable to report in. That the forces from Pullus had caught them.

In fact only one source had reported to her and was from the south east. Just like the rider from the walls he had charged full pelt to deliver his news to her. She now needed Leuan to finish before she broke the news to him.

Leuan stopped his speech, he spoke well, he had thought long about his words and believed it was what the room wanted to hear. The conniving was usually able to read the room. Not today though.

'My Prince, I agree we need strong leadership right now,' said a leading councilman as he got to his feet. He was an old round man with a gentle face and wispy grey hair. 'With your father's passing and apparent disappearance of Silos we will all follow your command.' Nods from men around the room backed him up so he continued. 'But we cannot have a coronation until your father is buried and Lachlan also, it is the law.' Most of the room nodded in agreement once more several voices backed the speaker. Leuan's eyes narrowed and he fought the urge to bite his lower lip by stealing a glance back at Catalina. Lord Wentwood stood next; he was the Guardian of the Golden tower much like Arian was in the Argentum. He was responsible for all the armies east of the Ridgeway with the exception of Lachlan and his Royal Guard. He sported thin white hair and a neat beard, he was a seasoned soldier now in his sixtieth year but still strong and skilled with the sword, no one could best him in his prime and few could now. He was responsible for training the Colossus who looked up to the knight in his youth, in Aurum only the king and his sons were more revered than the Golden knight.

'I agree with the learned gentleman my, Prince, you are next in line we will follow you word there is no need for further distraction until this danger has passed.'

'Desperate times call for desperate measures I feel, gentlemen.' Leuan responded. 'I want there to be no doubt as to the seriousness I take this threat.

'The population needs time to grieve for your beloved father we can't spare that time right now,' added another council member, Tradition in Ridgedale dictated that the new king could not be crowned till the old was properly buried in grand style. 'There is grief for your brother too.'

'Enough of this,' Leuan hissed, 'I'm in charge and I want the crown now!'

'We understand you grieve too…' said the first speaker.

'Silence!' The conniving cut him off pointed his finger at him angrily.

'You'd do well to remember you're not king yet, and you will need the support of the men present here,' put in Wentwood.

'Leave, all of you out!' yelled Leuan throwing up his hands in complete frustration. The room emptied with loud murmurs and many shaking their heads, the Prince's actions were put down to his grief, though, and Leuan had always been perceived as a little odd anyway. When they had left he slowly walked to his father's throne and sat in it for the first time since he was a young boy. Catalina went to him; his day wouldn't get any better.

Flames whipped around the Aerie while it burned, they leapt far into the red sky of dawn. The heat was intense at the top of the cliff, all the birds stood and watched helplessly nursing wounds, accept Apollo who remained unconscious after his battle with Magnus. Aves conceded that it was probably better he missed this it would have devastated him. A great groaning and part of the city fell deep into the abyss below. The little finches and sparrows in the trees the small animals that lived under them all were drawn to gaze on the inferno. At last the city which had stood for millennia and once sheltered hundreds gave up its struggle and succumbed, the blazing fires finally quenched by the waters of the Goodyson.

When Apollo came around a bit later every one of the great birds stood over or near him save Hcur There was a collective sigh of relief when he opened his eyes, fore the eagle might not have been leader in title but all looked up to him. For Apollo there was only one course of action now. He had to follow the cats, he was right in his belief that they could not have the sword under any circumstances. Their actions here were proof of that. The Great Eagle called into the air and a sparrow flew down and landed at his feet.

Venom the great dragon charged east as fast as her wings would carry her and pushed by some strong winds no doubt sent by the Dark Wizard to speed her along. The moths following just about kept up with her though she made no attempt to wait for them, if not for the winds they would have been long since left behind. She was exhausted by the time arrived at the canyon were she had left Marauder several days ago, she practically crossed the kingdom twice in that time and along with playing a large role in the battle at the Ridgegate. The bridge she burned was a broken mess as she expected. She looked around for anything to eat, something to give her some energy, she was so tired. Luckily she found cattle without too much effort.

Marauder should have headed roughly northwest to Aurum after the confrontation, she had found no sign that way which brought her back here. Those the Creeping Death chased were heading east so she decided to look that way for him. It wasn't long before she found him. Most of him anyway. Several moths immediately flew off to tell Pravus that one of his most important lieutenants had lost his head. Venom cursed herself; she should have stayed with him a bit longer until they had finished their quarry off. She should have stayed and finish off the prey rather than leave it to the

Assassin and that, along with Marauder's incompetence, had cost him his life. She could have torched the entire bridge with them on it and they wouldn't have been able to prevent her. Why hadn't she?

Those he chased were not to be found, they must have escaped. Should she chase them is that what Pravus would want? She decided to head on a bit further before heading to Aurum. Soon she settled on the cliff opposite were Eagles Aerie once was. The only signs that the city was once here were the piles of charred wood jutting out form the water below. Once again some moths flew back to Pullus.

Too many questions no one to interrogate for answers, she thought to herself. This place didn't concern her, anymore she decided; with Marauder dead it was time to head to Aurum.

The sparrow caught up with the foursome while they sailed. It landed on Hcur's shoulder and chirped away in his ear. He confirmed that a Puma was tailing them, Jak knew this already of course. It also broke the sad news that the Aerie was no more. The Hawk was crushed he could barely tell the others what had happened since they fled. Jak took over the paddle.

'I'm so sorry, my friend,' she said quietly.

'Magnus attacked them?' Austin repeated.

'He must really want the sword?' said Braydon rowing hard still.

'If Magnus has his heart set on the sword you can bet he won't stop till he has it,' answered Jak. Hcur said nothing, the little sparrow chirped one last time before flying off.

'You'll know him better than any of us how far will he go?' asked the archer.

'Judging by what we saw he'll chase us to our deaths.'

'Is he always that way?' Austin asked the cat next.

'He has a temper for sure but he is usually more restrained. Back there he was acting more like Jett. There's someone you don't want to get on the wrong side of. We had a fight he and I once, that's why I left the rock to get away from him. Fortunately I met Hcur and we've had some fun adventures which make up for missing home.'

They paddled in silence for a bit, Austin always looking up and back for any sign of Reon, none could be seen, though they knew he was there.

'I'm sorry about your home,' Austin said to the hawk after a while. 'It hurts to think of home at the moment I want to know what's happened to the silver city but I'm not sure if I can handle what's really happened to it on top of everything else going on.'

'Some people think that to be strong is to never feel pain.' The hawk spoke up at last. 'But a word of advice, Austin, in reality the strongest man understands the pain he feels and he accepts and learns from it.' He looked across the water at nothing in particular. Chajak broke the silence.

'We cats are a proud people once content to roam the lands in freedom, then many of us were made slaves, ultimately we were forced to settle on an small isle far from man. I think of Crosstree rock as my home, it always has been, but it is not so to all of us. Being forced there refocused my ancestors, they concentrated on what they had, like their honour. We became stronger warriors, Pravus knew this and tried to recruit us before crafting the Goblyns he now uses, because we spurned him. Honour is important to the cats.' The cheetah sighed. 'Recently, though, isolation has made Magnus somewhat bitter. He is the leader of warriors and he's looking to fight.'

The waters started to shallow out, trees hung out over the water on one side of the bank the other side was steep rock at this stretch of the river. A waterfall approached on that side, and then the waters turned and headed off northeast.

'The falls there signal the end of our journey by boat,' said the cheetah. 'From here on the Goodyson is more of a stream. We continue to Aurum by foot.'

Panic was now almost widespread through the Ridgedale's greatest city. It was soon common knowledge that the army had suffered a crushing defeat at the Ridgegate. most folk were shocked by the news stunned that this could happen seemingly out of the blue, after all the king had hidden anything about war from them for so long. While the locals tried to digest all this more bad news presented itself. What remained of the army that had fled from the walls, hoping it was now safe in the capital. Close behind it came the Goblyns. Those few that thought of fleeing the city in the faint hope of finding somewhere safer now had no choice but to remain.

The darksiders charged straight at the city, not even resting themselves from there chase. No strategy was needed by order of Malice. Their only mission was to spread fear and panic in the city. And they succeeded in doing that in spectacular fashion. The men just arrived from the Ridgegate exhausted as they were, called on to form ranks once again. Backed now by the city's guards and reinforcements of their own they lined up just outside the limits of the new town. Archers took out most of the Goblyns as they flooded in west across the Plains of Luca the rest crashed into a sea of shields and swinging swords. Blades clashed and more blood was split. Folk of the new town abandoned their homes and business to take shelter behind the age old golden walls. The battle was quite short and the Goblyns were destroyed, only six lives were lost by the defenders. But all knew now that it was just the beginning. Perhaps the beginning of the end.

After dismissing his meeting Leuan then learned about Catalina's news. His mood got no better. A trusted though often unheard from agent had sent word that four men were headed to the city. Leuan read the small parchment again and reread it over and over. The note read;

Four sail up the Goodyson
All armed strange attire
Two look... odd.

'Odd!' seethed Leuan once more. 'What the devil does that mean?'

'I know no more than what the message says, my prince,' answered Catalina curtly.

'What kind of clowns work for you, my dear?' he demanded. She rubbed her temples.

'What we have to do is read further into the message lord.'

He shook his hands in his head and sat back into Leland's throne.

'Go on.'

'First who would sail up the Goodyson? There are no soldiers stationed by the river by my information, no towns or villages out that way. The Goodyson flows from the Forbidden Canyon once again no men should be around there. Why would four men be coming from that way?' Leuan's hands now came together and touched the tip of his nose. Catalina continued 'Old tales tell of strange beasts that lived in that region.'

'They are very old tales indeed.'

'The message says two looked funny.' The intelligencer continued, 'who may come from the forbidden lands looking strange?' The conniving remained silent. 'I recall another old rumour that says your father is the reason that region is out of bounds. The kings law forbids anyone from going there even the army only patrols its borders.'

'It wasn't my father but a king many years before him made that law. He told me once when I was young why those lands are forbidden. I never believed him.'

'May I ask what he said my prince?'

'I have a feeling that as a person with your knowledge you know exactly what he spoke of.'

'At one time I had many eyes watching borders to those lands, once I heard the rumours I was determined to verify them. I stopped sending men to explore when they failed to return. Then I saw one.' She spoke slowly.' I say I as I happened by lucky chance to be there at the time, and I rarely leave Aurum's walls, your grace. I could only describe it as a cross between bird and man.'

'So what the old man told me was true.'

'Oh yes. It saw us and quickly disappeared. If I could describe it I would say it walked like a man but it was covered in brown feathers it had a big beak and large eyes. And it carried a large silver shield on its back it resembled wings.

'So it was armed.'

'Indeed. No other was sighted for considerable time. Then those spotted were always hooded and elusive.'

'So the question remains,' mused Leuan. 'Why are they coming here now?'

Chapter XII: Many Battles

There was no doubt that Reon was catching them, the cats were swift on foot especially in pursuit. Chajak could have lost him she was certain, but her companions even the Hawk was just not as quick. Whereas she was always confident that the green assassin wouldn't catch them she was convinced the Puma would and soon. On the river they had maintained a good pace and had even pulled away some from their chaser, but now they had left the boat he was gaining that lost ground. They jogged through a small wood the ground was soft and Jak couldn't help turning every now and then and looking at the track behind them. There was no mistaking the footprints they were leaving behind; she shook her head they were making it even easier for Reon.

The wood was light and made up of large thick trees that had many branches with bright red and gold leaves. Jak called the group to a stop when they neared a tree that was in the middle of their path. It was the largest tree in sight and Austin thought it almost looked like the gallows tree outside of tombstone.

'This is no good, friends, we won't get to Aurum being chased,' she said. Braydon and Austin bent over trying to regain their breath. Hcur looked to the sky head almost cocked then he took a quick drink from his new flask. All now carried more than they had before arriving at the Aerie. The fresh provisions were welcome but still an added weight to carry along with the weapons, Austin especially struggled to keep a good pace.

'You're right, he's catching us.' He looked up at the giant tree in front of them. 'But I have a plan,' he continued.

They all climbed up the tree it had five huge branches even spaced apart like a star about twelve metres up. Each limb itself was huge and ran almost level for a good distance one of these ran back directly above the path they had come up. Hcur perched on this branch so he could see Reon approach, the others took a different branch each. They could easily move away from the thick truck and hide in the red leaves further along.

It wasn't long before Hcur saw the Puma race up the path and underneath him, he ran past the tree and quickly stopped. Scanning the ground then all around for the tracks that now halted. His searching brought him back to the tree he walked around it. Hcur whistled and Reon immediately looked up. And stepped a few paces towards his direction. He couldn't see anyone but the Hawk knew that he realised they were up there. The hawk whistled again to draw him away from the others, Reon drew a sword from over his shoulder eyes darting everywhere searching for a target in the leaves.

The bird caught him completely unawares. He dropped from the tree like a stone feet together arms apart. He seemed to fall in slow motion but the cat below had no time to react. His boots landed squarely on Reon's chest and the cat was knocked hard into the dirt. Hcur picked himself up and immediately went to check his foe. The blow and stunned the Puma who was now unconscious.

'Austin get down here I need something!' he called out.

So the group continued to Aurum, Reon now tied to a tree unable to follow, Austin, though, was upset to leave his father's rope behind even though he understood it was necessary.

Hcur's route took them north past Caster the eastern most of the Green mountains then they would turn west and head to the capital. A day out from the Aerie and Hcur remained quiet speaking little and keeping his distance behind the group. They walked now unable to jog any more, but Jak made them keep as brisk a pace as possible they even ate on the move. They walked a narrow but open path, trees lined the way either side, or it ran mostly straight climbing slightly as they were leaving the uneven terrain of the canyon. Austin and Braydon chatted as they trekked.

'I hope our friend's mood improves,' Braydon said, 'he is not good to us in his current state.'

'I know how he feels, he's just lost his home and is being chased by people he considered friends.'

'He is a remarkable being, Jak, too, he has the heart of a warrior and the head of a scholar. Strength and wisdom are valuable friends but he needs to focus right now. He would tell you the same.'

'He'll come around I'm sure.'

'I hope so because our destiny awaits us in Aurum,' Braydon looked down on the sword Austin carried, 'and it won't be easy to achieve.'

'I thought my destiny would be decided on this journey, I guess it has—'

'Not so you still have a role to play I'm certain of it, Austin. Remember often one finds one's destiny just where one hides from it.'

'What does that mean?' asked Austin.

'Well I don't really know,' Braydon laughed, 'I'm just trying to hand out kingly advice I suppose, and I heard Hcur say it to Jak back at the Aerie. Her destiny was to turn her back on her race to support you,' he looked ahead to her sadly. 'We need to support her like she has us.' Austin nodded his agreement. 'The sword is so important now our nation is split Austin, it has been since the rule of the four Tyrants, Leland hasn't been able to unite us properly again, the real power is with the knights that the king ignores to his cost perhaps. The Knights will follow the sword.'

As Braydon was speaking Austin saw a sparrow fly low overhead and straight to Hcur. He lifted his arm and it landed and cheeped excitedly away while the hawk listened. Finally it flew back to the blue sky and Hcur jogged up to his fellows, Jak fell back in line with them.

'What news old friend?' she inquired.

'Events are taking a turn for the worse it seems. The dark wizard's forces have pushed past the Ridgegate and are marching on Aurum as we speak.

'Impossible the gate cannot be breached,' said Braydon astonished, Austin would have agreed he had seen the Botley Fortifications several times and they looked impregnable.

'They were none the less, but there is more. The Constant is dead, as is the Colossus,' Braydon stopped and put his hands on his head, Austin put his over his mouth.

'What does this mean?' asked the boy, 'our journey has been for nothing, there'll be a new king now anyway! It's all been a waste of time' he threw his back against a tree and slid down to a crouch shaking his head.

'Not so, Austin, Civitas Aurum still needs defending from Sinister,' said Jak 'a new king still need to be crowned.' She grabbed his shoulders and pulled him back up. Something then took her attention. She paused and looked up her senses scanning everything around her. 'Take cover!' she yelled and as she charged at Austin pushing him backwards in to the trees. Then a massive Silhouette blocked out the sun for an instant as it flew past.

Venom had flown over some bird like men, a dozen she guessed, any other time she would have stopped and had some fun, but she needed to get to Aurum now the time was passing by. Then she soared over a great pack of large cats charging the same way as her, were they running from the birds? They must have numbered some hundreds and were in a hurry. A few launched arrows at her but she didn't slow. No time for them but remember this place she thought, I must come back here when the taste of men gets tiresome.

Then she came across Marauder's prey. She was flying so fast she almost didn't spot them, she circled back around where they had hidden themselves. These she would stop for she decided Pravus wouldn't mind, she had time enough to find out what was so important about them.

Austin saw the dragon swoop back it flew low looking for them, it looked a terrifying sight, with its three horns and large spiky tail. It landed on all fours on the path close to them. Shrubs and ferns hid them from its crimson red eyes. Jak pushed his head down further trying to keep him out of sight, Braydon was close flat on his chest, Hcur dived to the other side of the path and Austin couldn't see him. He looked back over at the great beast it seemed to be sniffing the air for them. Jak's eyes never lifted off it, she was crouching and Austin knew she was working out the best way, if any, to engage it.

'Come out little things,' Venom roared. Smoke drifted from her nostrils when she paused. 'Or I'll burn this wood to the ground and you with it.' No one made a move so the dragon raised her head while flame erupted from her jaws; several treetops close to her were instantly alight. 'Last chance!'

Then something else caught her attention, she spat a long burst of flame down the path Austin couldn't see at what or who from his vantage point. Jak kept her paw on him, 'it's Magnus,' the cheetah said not taking her eyes off Venom, 'he's caught up.'

Magnus had five hundred cats charging with him. They saw the beast overtake them; the king of Lions wondered where it had come from and what its reason was for being in these parts. Very soon they saw it again in the distance circling above a part of the wood, Magnus knew why it was here now. It wanted the sword also. And it had found it. The beast dropped from the sky and landed, Magnus slowed his pace and ordered his fellows to fan out either side, to out flank the beast. He saw the creature torch some of the wood close by itself. It would not take Custos Ferrum the Guardian's sword was his. He snarled over his shoulder at Jett who nodded and growled back, then charged at the Dragon.

The creature blew more fire into the woods, trees blazed all around them. 'You have friends I see.' Called out Venom, her head darted from tree to tree searching everywhere. The Sorcerer wants to be your friend, too, only he doesn't play very nice. Give yourselves up and I'll tell him to make your deaths quick. Well, quicker anyway.' More flames were aimed at the cats who raced down the path. Jak now pointed to various spots in the woods, she said nothing and Austin wondered what she was doing until she saw Braydon looking over and nodding. He looked again to where Jak pointed and he saw it. The woods were alive. Movement swept towards them. He rubbed his eyes and realised it was the Cats they had been found. Austin felt he was stuck between a rock and a hard place, and still Jak kept him low. Then he heard a roar from the path, a host of Cats charged at the dragon led by Jett, Austin recognised the fearsome tiger, until the dragon was here he thought Jett to be the scariest being he had met. He didn't want to meet the Dark Lord. Jett rolled for cover other cats weren't so quick, At least not as fast as flames that burned them. More cats charged from Hcur's side of the path, more flames meet them. Venom swung her great tail to greet them as well, it brushed them aside effortlessly. Braydon sat up and let loose some arrows following the lead of some of the cats, they bounced harmlessly off the dragons scales though. Jett was now close and swung his sword at the dragons head, it struck her and she flinched, then pierced him with her evil eyes. Then she pierced him again – this time with her tail. The spikes impaled the hulking tiger. More and more charged, weapons drawn, but no weapon could break her armour. Jak leapt up to attack also, Braydon still fired his arrows. Crouching Austin could see Hcur, mace in hand, swatting at the beast in vain. Venom seemed to chuckle like she was amused – was this all they could do to her? She lifted her head and drew a circle of fire in the blue sky then brought the flame down on those around her. All scattered. Now Magnus could be seen charging down the path, like Jett before him he roared as he went for the creature's head. Austin was compelled to reach for his sword as the Lion swung at the horns on the dragons head. Austin drew the Guardian's sword and stood; Venom lunged at Magnus and wrapped her jaws around him. Hcur saw Austin race towards the beast, he yelled out to him to stop. Jak saw him now too; she threw her arms wide hoping he would halt. The dragon shifted her weight to her back feet and prepared to take to the air. Then something stopped her and her left side foreleg went numb. Austin had plunged his sword hilt deep into her neck. She dropped Magnus and tried to look around at the source of her pain, but her neck wouldn't allow it. Where all other swords had failed the Guardian's sword succeeded. It had breached the dragon's scales. Austin still clutched it tightly, unable or unwilling to let go of it. Magnus looked up, an expression of relief, fear and confusion across his face. Venom slumped onto her belly unable to do anything about the sword in her neck, all her strength failed her she would have flown to safety if she had the might and regrouped to fight another day. The cats growled and roared around the dragons prone frame now, Jak included, many tried thrusting their swords at her also but no more penetrated the hard scales.

'My thanks, boy,' rumbled Magnus, 'but the beast needs putting out of its misery and our swords won't do it.'

Austin was unsure what he meant. Jak approached him and put her paw on his shoulder, instinctively Austin pulled the Sword out of Venom's neck, and as he did so, as if by some reflex, her giant wings stretched out one last time knocking several cats over close by. Braydon reached Austin and took the sword; Austin did not attempt to stop him. Braydon raised the sword high, not a mark or stain from the dragon was on it. It shone in the sky the sun reflecting off the silver blade, then he brought it down on the beast's neck, its head dropped to the floor, its body slumped further. Unseen to all in the far from the battle a small eclipse of black moths set of east to Pullus.

'What now, your grace? Do we fight again?' Braydon asked the king of Lions as he handed Austin back the sword. Austin quickly put it back in its scabbard, and turned his body from the king slightly. He looked around at all the cats that surrounded them; there would be no escape this time. Hcur and Jak gathered close to Austin. Looking at him Magnus finally spoke,

'You saved my life, son of Arian.' He gritted his teeth. 'And for that I am in your debt.'

'You can pay that debt immediately by releasing your claim on his sword,' suggested Hcur,' the king just snarled.

'We have received word that the enemy is near Aurum, we have to get there soon before my people fall,' Braydon spoke with urgency.

'I care not about your people,' Magnus said quietly.

'They are all that is stopping Pravus from marching further east towards your lands,' Austin added surprising himself with the confidence in his voice.

'Join us, my king,' pleaded Jak. Magnus looked around, at the fires still burning the charred remains of his fallen comrades and finally at the dragon carcass.

'I won't follow you,' he growled at last. 'But I will follow the sword.'

Chapter XIII: A Final Stand

Good news and bad come hand in hand Pravus thought. He was thrilled by the victory brought to him by Malice; but this was soured by failures elsewhere. Firstly his raptors had failed him and Venom had destroyed them, what few he had left he had now sent to his general. Then his moths returned and told him news of Marauder's death. This was grievous news indeed, he had no love for the assassin, or his cousin for that matter, but he was an important tool and had a vital role to play in the golden city. He was to sneak in and bring out the king's son's head. News had reached him of Leland's death, but that did not change his plans in any way, he still wanted Leuan's head. His royal father could not suffer, so the present royals must suffer in his place. Lachlan was ash, Leland beyond his reach. He would have to send Venom after the prince later.

Something else bothered him now though. What had the Creeping Death died for? He was chasing a boy and his animal friends across the lands to what end? The Sorcerer decided he had to find out why. In a dark room in his citadel he gestured at the floor and a stone slab rose up. It was black as tar and what little light was in the chamber was absorbed by it. Pravus lay on it and cast his mind over the kingdom of his birth, across the many miles to the canyon where Marauder fell. There it was at the bottom of a ravine, eyes open mouth slightly ajar, pale as the moon. Resting in a tuft of grass inches away from the flowing Goodyson was the assassins head. The Dark Lord focused hard on it, he was shaking as he lay there. The colour drained away from the lifeless eyes on the head, milky pools all that was left, then images appeared across them. Pravus focused on them intently. He saw many images in those eyes, he saw the chase, he saw a cart and three men, he saw Venom lift him up high, then a fall from a bridge and a hard landing. The dragon torched a bridge, a sword made of pure silver, the assassin fighting a cat. The sword again.

Pravus sat up then stood and placed his hands on the slab. A large old leather book appeared in between his pale hands. A flick of his fingers and the book opened on the page was a sketching of a sword. It was the same one that his assassin saw. Marauder had been chasing the Guardian's sword.

All this time the sword still existed Pravus had thought it lost centuries ago, like everyone he knew the tales that it would unite a kingdom and the rest. The sword that the Phoenix gave his father all those years ago. It matters not he decided it's too late for Ridgedale. It changes nothing in the grand plan at worst it is merely a delay. His army was marching east even as he sat. No nothing could stop him he was the tide and the tide stopped for no one.

Before they continued to Aurum Magnus insisted that the fallen be put on a pyre, the thought of leaving them was something he couldn't bear. He also left three behind to oversee the dead and then to strip the dragon, he wanted its bones they would prove invaluable. Over four hundred armed Cats, two men and one hawk travelled as quickly as they could over the rocky ground. They were marching around the mountain known as Castor and the path was uneven. The ground sloped sharply in many places grass and large grey rocks were all that could be seen by Austin. It seemed like forever since they had taken a rest and Austin was struggling, but the Cats showed no signs of slowing down. Braydon looked at Austin.

'Come on, lad, there's a long way to go yet.' He laughed and if he was tired Austin couldn't see it.

'I'm tired, Braydon, I can't go on and go to war feeling like this, I've nothing to give,' Braydon put his hand on Austin's arm and said,

'Losers quit when they're tired, boy, winners quit when they've won. We've a city to save and we won't stop till we're there.' With that he said no more and Austin dropped a few paces behind him. He thought that Braydon reminded him of his father somewhat. He was loyal strong and determined and had some wisdom about him, he would make a good king and Austin would stand by him.

A full three days after killing the dragon Civitas Aurum came into sight; its tallest golden tower crept up from over a hill. It was the Green peak and following it was the plains of Luca, three miles now separated them from the golden city. They had rushed past two villages on the way Castors Shadow and Hess Wall which sat by the river Hess. Neither Hcur nor Jak wore their hoods any longer as Magnus and the cats didn't as and they were soon to announce themselves to man, why hide anymore? Magnus called his men to a halt, Austin immediately collapsed to the floor exhausted.

'The pride will stay here; we five will go and see what the city has to say,' spoke the king of cats.

'And if we're welcome,' added Jak with a grin. Braydon nodded and looked at Austin, Hcur and Jak in turn. All were nervous about what reception would meet them. They stared over the Green peak the city, in wondrous glory, came into view. Just past it, away in the distance to the left was a sea of black. The sea was alive rippling; there was no mistaking the dark prince's army. Behind it was snaking a line of goblin's still arriving at the Ridge Mountains, no one would venture a guess as to how many could be seen.

'Any regrets about coming?' Braydon asked them, he tried to chuckle.

'A word of advice, archer, never regret, if it's good it's wonderful. If it's bad it's an experience,' said the hawk.

'You won't learn from you experience if your dead,' added Magnus gravely. They continued in silence.

Catalina raced back to Leuan she barged into the throne room and there he was there in his father's grand throne. He was alone, he had dismissed everyone one around him. Sent away to defend the city, every man young or old and every boy big enough to hold a weapon had been sent to join the troops. They covered the cities towering walls, the new town outside had been abandoned everything that could be taken was, buildings that could be levelled were, as much wood and straw was taken as they could manage. They didn't want the enemy to burn it around them, though they could no longer stop them. The Goblyns' ranks had been swelling for hours but no attack so far; was the dark wizards plan, some wondered, not to fight the city but to stave it?

'My man on the east wall just sent this.' Catalina bowed as she handed a scrap of parchment over. Leuan read it with mild annoyance.

'They're here so soon?'

'Crossing the plains as we speak, my king. Shall I order riders out to great them?'

'No,' said Leuan flatly.

'Then what is to be done with them?'

'We can spare no men but such important visitors do deserve a welcome, so they shall have a royal one. Send for Wentwood to meet me at the east gate.'

Austin could see no sign of life in the city as they neared, he had been to Aurum a few times and the place always seemed to heave even from a distance. Then he realised the buildings now resembled ruins the place was almost a ghost town. The Goblyns were hidden from view now he took some comfort in that, but he knew they were far beyond the walls on the far side of the city. He could make out many men though up on the massive walls, soldiers he knew they were ready for the battle. He looked up at the cities great towers they reminded him of the silver tower back home, he wondered it seen still stood after the dark army had poured through it. Then movement ahead caught his eye, five men on horses rode out to greet them.

The Knight Wentwood led the way Austin had met him once long ago, he had been a guest of his father. He wore elegant golden armour and a red cloak. He was followed by the prince who now wore a gold chest plate and a woman; they were flanked to two soldiers. The Knight rode right up to them before halting. His confusion at seeing Hcur and the cats was evident.

'What brings you to the golden tower in this dark time? Speak now.'

Braydon stepped forward. 'I am Braydon son of Brandon. I formerly served the Royal Army as an archer. I travel with the son of Arian of Argentum and three companions I have come to trust with my life. They are Magnus king of Crosstree Rock, Chajak also of the rock and Hcur of Eagles Aerie. I am here in the city's darkest hour to unite our people.' He reached out his hand to Austin who after a pause drew the Guardian's sword and presented it to Braydon.

'Braydon?' One of the soldiers looked shocked. He was a round short man with ginger whiskers and a red face. 'Your Grace this man should be dead by rights. Convicted of treason when he struck me, allow me to bring you his head.'

'I wouldn't do that,' snarled Jak.

'Why did you strike our Captain Ionne?' asked Leuan with the trace of a smile. Braydon offered his hands and said with a shrug,

'The captain's an ass who deserved it. We have more important matters to worry about.'

'Why do you bring them here?' said Wentwood nodding at the Cats and Hcur.

'We are long friends of the silver tower, and now count Braydon as a friend, too,' said Hcur. Disbelief was written over the knight's face along with the Ionne and the other.

'Lord Arian knew of—'

'So here you are then,' Leuan interrupted. He dismounted and approached Braydon as did Wentwood. 'That is a fine sword do you offer it to me?'

'I do not, your father was guilty of allowing the Goblyn terror to grow in the west I've come with the sword to deal with that threat and take the crown.'

'Treason!' cried Leuan. Wentwood reached for his own sword but did not draw it yet.

'It's the firebird's sword you all know the lore. I have not come for your blood you need just step aside,' continued Braydon.

'Do you think I will?' spat Leuan he looked them all over with disgust. 'A ragtag crew you are, animals and one of Ionne's disgraced archers. He looked at Austin. 'And you? You're the child of Arian, what a shame such an honourable man's son should be arrested for treason.'

'No one's been arrested yet,' pointed out Hcur dryly, 'nor will they.'

'And why not?' sneered the conniving 'Am I just to roll over and hand you the crown that I've waited my whole life for. My dear father, your king, has not long left us and I'm to honour his memory giving up everything he worked so long for. No I won't do it.' Wentwood now looked uneasy he was staring at the weapon in Braydon's hands.

'What of the legend, though, my liege? *Returned a new King will finally stand.*'

'You fool! I'm the new king the sword has returned even though he has it!' Leuan pointed his slender fingers at Braydon. 'Give me the sword,' he demanded. Braydon pointed it at him in return.

'The sword is mine, people will flock to my banner when I reveal it to them. And together we will smash the evil lord and create a new Ridgedale.' Braydon spoke with passion and authority.

'Wentwood take the sword for me,' shouted Leuan.

'Do as your king commands,' pressed Catalina, the knight threw her a dark look. They all now started finger pointing and quarrelling, a war of words over a crown and a blade, Austin knew it could go on forever like this or turn nasty in a heartbeat. He wanted an end to this squabble quickly he knew the priority for them all should be the defence of the capital and suddenly he had a thought.

'What if the sword deems you unworthy?' All stopped and looked at him.

'There is no one more worthy than I!' yelled Leuan.

'Braydon why don't you hand the prince the Phoenix Sword.'

'Do not call me prince, boy, I am a king!' screamed Leuan.

'We shall see,' he answered.

'Austin?' questioned Braydon, but the boy just nodded back with encouragement.

'Perhaps you do owe him that, friend,' added Hcur; the archer shot a glance back at the hawk and took a deep breath. Leuan extended his arm and opened his hand eager for it. Braydon who was still pointing it at the conniving gritted his teeth and tossed the sword lightly in the air. He caught it near the blade gingerly and offered the hilt to Leuan with narrow eyes. Leuan went to receive the sword but an unseen force prevented him from doing so his hand stopped short and he could not make it reach the blade. At the same time Braydon was unable to hand Custos Ferrum over, he held it firm and he couldn't push further towards the prince. Leuan struggled for almost a minute but they remained an inch apart.

'What is this trickery?' demanded Leuan pulling back.

'I would say the sword deems you unworthy,' suggested Hcur. Austin nodded his agreement with a grin. Even Jak had a little smile, the king of lions remained impassive.

'Join us, sir,' Braydon offered.

'Ionne go back to the city call the men bring as many as you need to bring; we have necks to hang.' The chubby man looked startled.

'Stop there,' ordered Wentwood before Ionne could turn.

'What?' gasped Leuan in disbelief.

'The sword didn't pick you, you cannot command the men,' the Golden knight said.

'No one will put any stock into this fairy-tale!'

'I do,' said the knight and with that he dropped to one knee and bowed in front of Braydon.

'Thank you for your trust, Sir.' Braydon turned to Leuan, 'We're going to the city, stand aside.'

'I won't move I still have my army.'

Braydon just laughed at him. 'So do I,' then he winked at the Lion. Magnus finally grinned and let out a ferocious growl so loud it echoed around the city walls. Men on Aurum's walls covered their ears and wondered what manner of beast could make such a noise, even the Goblyns paused while assembling their ranks. Leuan had a face of sheer terror as Austin and his friends looked back to the Green peak. A Jaguar came into view at first then another cat very soon the crest of the hill was lined with cats marching towards them.

'No!' screamed Leuan as he lunged for the sword but Magnus caught him and threw him away as if he were garbage. The would-be king scrambled to his knees and hissed at them.

'This isn't over, not by a long way, Ridgedale is mine!' yelled Leuan, Jak snarled at him. Catalina raced over with his horse and he climbed on. 'This isn't over!' He repeated, and then they turned and raced of north.

As the many cats neared, Wentwood turned to Ionne and told him to ride back and say that some new allies were here. Braydon then gifted the knight the *Sword of the Moon* for his trust. Wentwood recognised the blade as Viridis steel, forged in a forgotten land that was now known as Pullus. Swords made in Viridis were reputed to never lose their edge, to stay sharp for all time, but that was before the volcanos turned the lands to Ash. Braydon led the march back to the east gate as he neared he raised Custos Ferrum up high for all on the wall to see. Word was soon spreading through the city that the Guardian's sword had returned and with it a new champion. Everyone was boosted by the news 'it's a good sign' they said with spirits cheered. Minds were further distracted from the impending battle when people caught sight of the creatures who accompanied the champion, new friends to help smash the Goblyns. All saw this as a good omen, cheering broke out around the walls and soon Braydon was greeted with applause as he continued his way through the city. He climbed steps up to the wall and circled half the city till he was at the west gate and facing the enemy. He passed no emotionless face; many had the look of awe at him, his sword and allies, others had looks of shock, while some openly wept. But a new defiance was evident in all already. He accepted some armour a golden breast plate and steel for his shoulders, and instructed Austin to wear some also, Jak and Hcur declined. While he donned it a song broke out and was sung by many one that had not been heard for years in the Golden walls of Civitas Aurum.

One day it shall return
The Guardian's silver sword dancing again
With it comes hope anew
The First's lost blade with see us through

After the verse had been sung for several minutes it was drowned out by a deafening racket. The goblyn's started beating drums, shields and whatever else could find, slowly and steadily dum, dum, dum dum, dum. In the city all thought turned once again to the enemy they faced. As Austin and his friends looked out to the west toward the dark forces lining up against them they all realised what threat they were up against. They knew Pravus was a danger, he always had been after all, but now his army was here and it had crushed Argentum and the Ridgegate to get here.

'Are all the cities defences ready?' Braydon asked Wentwood.

'As ready as can be,' was the reply 'Catapults stand by as do the Archers and spears on the walls. Hot oil also waits for them when they reach our feet.'

'Will that be enough?' asked Hcur. Wentwood didn't reply but his silence was answer enough Austin thought.

'We will take the initiative,' spoke Braydon loudly so all around could hear. 'I call for fifty volunteers to join me, preferably those who can shoot.'

'What do you plan?' quizzed the hawk.

'To surprise the goblin's to hit them first rather than wait for them to strike,' was Braydon's answer.

'Right, by doing what?' asked Hcur again.

'Come and find out.' No arrows could reach the dark prince's ranks from the current distance so Braydon planned simply to get closer and take out as many as he could before the enemy charged back. Then Braydon and his volunteers would run like the wind back to the safety of the wall. Braydon wanted it to be a statement he explained, a sign he was willing to sacrifice himself for the folk he would rule. Hcur and Jak got their hands on some bows and joined him, Austin went also; where they went he would go too. Some of Braydon's old friends from the Royal army were the first to join him; they greeted him with back slapping and banter. Soon he had more than enough volunteers needed for his plan and they left the old city and entered the empty remains of the new town. Braydon led the way once more, from the west gate along a straight path to the edge of the city.

Braydon planted Custos Ferrum in the soil and knelt behind it. The wall of noise form ahead was almost deafening now as the Goblyns tried to intimidate their foes. To many behind Braydon it was working, fear was once again rife throughout the city. He was aware that Austin was now behind him as he put his quiver over the hilt of the sword.

'I'm scared, Bray,' said Austin loudly to be heard, he was trembling. Braydon laughed.

'That's no way to talk to a king, lad.' He laughed again as he raised his bow setting his arrow. He looked at the quiver fourteen were there, he nodded behind him and all readied their arrows as well. He looked at the enemy all he could see was a wall of black, they would soon be a few shorter in number. 'Not until my command' he said. The he let fire his arrow, just over seventeen seconds later and fifteen Goblyn's collapsed in front of their ranks. Braydon raised the Guardian's sword and gave the command. More arrows flew and more Goblyn's hit the dirt, there were so many that very few missed a target.

Malice laughed from his position. As at the walls he had set up camp on a hillock so he could see over the top of his forces. He saw a number of men approach and fire their arrows; it mattered not to the general he knew they run out of arrows before he ran out of Goblyn's. But they had made the first move so now was time to retaliate.

The ground shock when the darksiders charged. All arrows had been spent and now Braydon wanted to charge them back, meet them head on. Hcur grabbed him and told him he was being foolish reminding him that was not the plan, while seven of his archer friend drew short swords and charged off anyway. Jak was sorely tempted to go with them but decided to help Hcur drag Braydon back to the safety. The seven men were quickly drowned in a sea of black, trampled by countless evil feet. Austin reached the walls ahead of most he was out of breath when he ran past the gate. But Braydon didn't stop there with him, he ran right back up to the top of the walls and demanding more arrows.

Wentwood had already given the order to fire and arrows rained off the wall into the enemy. Soon the catapults fired also flaming missiles hit the enemy ranks and took out many, but more continued to swarm around the city. They used catapults of their own and returned arrows, but they had nowhere near the same effect. The massive army surrounded the walls; soon anything that remained of the old town was trampled into dust by thousands of Goblyn boots. Braydon guessed they must have numbered two hundred thousand, Wentwood believed less than half that number was in city. Hot oil poured down the wall onto the Goblyn's and their losses grew, but they still had many to throw at the city.

For an hour or so it seemed like a stalemate had set in, the city took relatively few casualties while inflicting many, but a few still realised the Goblyn's still held the upper hand. Braydon and his men had nowhere to go even if the dark forces couldn't break the walls they could ultimately starve the city with time.

Malice wanted to conquer the city, though, like he crushed his opposition across the nation; he ordered great Battering rams to be wheeled up. One went to the west gate one to the south and another to the north. Dragged by the biggest Goblyn's, they were massive wooden trunks reinforced with steel protected by a wooden canopy. The Goblyn's swung them with all their might under fire from the walls, but the gates stood.

A whip crack filled the air, it sounded to Austin like a bullwhip in the courtyard back home as it echoed though the skies. A billowing cloud of blue smoke rose from behind the Goblyn ranks. When it settled Pravus stood, sword in hand, a thin silver crown shining in the late afternoon sun. He looked around taking in all around him. The arrows stopped flying the rams stopped their attack on the doors. A young man, and he was a man not a solider, fled from the walls not far from Austin. He didn't notice it happen, though, all eyes were drawn to the appearance of the dark prince. He spoke and his harsh raspy voice was heard by all.

'I am here to take what was denied me before your ancestors were even born. I am Pravus you will learn now truly why my name has bought terror for five hundred years. I'm not some bastard son looking to get one over my other siblings. I'm not some beggar off the streets trying to make a name for myself. I am Pravus I was the son of Ridgedale's father. I won't dignify his name by uttering it out loud. I am older than the nation itself and it is my birth right and long have I waited.'

'Your words fall on deaf ears here, lord of evil,' shouted Braydon, 'you may choose to believe them, there may even be some truth to your bile, but know that we will not surrender our freedom to your iron grip.' Austin noticed that Jak and Hcur nodded their approval at this.

'Fools,' mocked Pravus. He clenched his fists and pulled them to his chest, then he opened his hands towards the west gate and it seemed to all that something tore through the air.

The great wall of Aurum cracked slightly, the wall shook and the men on it held its sides for fear of falling. Pravus lowered his head and balled his fist again. Another whip crack and the rent he had made grew larger still then the great west gate, a gate that had stood for almost six hundred years since the days of Luca the First slowly fell down. The Goblyns didn't wait for the dust to settle they poured straight through the opening. To their shock though they were met by over four hundred armed cats roaring at them.

The cats bared their teeth and charged meeting the Goblyn's head on; they were closely followed by the men of the city. The sounds of clashing steel echoed around the buildings in the city as weapons clashed. Wentwood was impressed with his new sword it glided through the air reaping Goblyn's by the number. Chajak's swords danced so fast they were rarely seen be it apart or when she had them joined, her opponents' bodies strewn all about her. Hcur's mighty mace could not cut through the air like a sword but with the force behind its swing the hawk left many a Goblyn in the dirt. Magnus roared often, a low sound that came from his gut; it terrified all around him even his allies. Throughout the battle he would often grab his foes by the throat and pick them up one handed squeezing the breath out of them before tossing them aside.

Pravus watched as the carnage raged ahead of him he was joined by his general and the Goblyn shield.

'Shall I order more into the city my lord?' asked Malice, many thousands of foes still stood behind them drums beating a haunting soundtrack to the contest.

'No let them break out let them come to me,' replied sinister.

'They won't leave the walls they'll just hide in the city it is their only chance.'

'No they'll come; they'll want to test that sword.'

'What sword?' asked Malice puzzled, Pravus didn't reply. As he predicted the forces defending Aurum soon conquered what Goblyn's had entered the city and Braydon and Magnus led the charge out of the cracked wall. Wentwood counselled caution but the Braydon knew victory wouldn't come from hiding in the city, their only chance was to take the fight to the enemy. Hcur and Jak agreed reluctantly knowing it would cost many lives, Magnus just wanted to fight.

Austin had remained high up on the walls at first targeting the dark army with his bow, but when Braydon exited to what little was left of the new town he stayed as close to him as he could. He still fired away he knew he couldn't match strength with the creatures by attacking them head on but he was quick with his bow. He soon got used to the fact he had to pull arrows from the fallen as his own had long been spent. His bow fingers were raw and starting to blister but he did not stop. A great call was heard from the east, like birdsong only louder and more sombre. Austin strained to see through the mass of bodies what it was – it was Hcur who told him.

'The winged warriors arrive!' the hawk shouted.

'What?' Austin said still searching.

'Back on the peak, it's Apollo.' Sure enough the twelve birds stood atop the Greenpeak and surveyed the scene ahead of them. Apollo greatest of eagles had already made the decision that the Cats' treachery could be put aside, but only for now. This battle ahead of them needed to be settled first. With a war cry he led his companions to the closest enemies.

The fighting continued for what seemed to Austin like an age then he saw Magnus charge at a figure on the edge of the battle. The king of the cats had slowly been ploughing a path towards the dark prince the dead littered the floor around him. Then he saw his chance and he charged, though Malice blocked his path. Sinister ordered his general stand aside though, and the Defender's sword of Magnus clashed with the blade of Acerbus. Pravus faced his foe calmly side on never with two hands on his weapon; the Lion swung his weapon wildly unable to grasp how the dark lord was blocking his attacks.

The birds' arrival had caused a momentary distraction but their numbers were too few to worry Malice for long; he had now had decided to dirty his own hands, his sullied blade caught a lynx unawares from behind and the cat fell. It did not go unnoticed by Hcur, though, whose great mace sent the general crashing to the dirt. Malice climbed back to his feet, his skeletal armour now bent. He attacked Hcur, his sword deflecting off the hawk's wing like shield, in the meantime Jak was picking off the troops of his Goblyn shield. She claimed the lives of all the Goblyn's that wore blood red. Malice attacked Hcur with a fury forcing the hawk backwards with every strike, but he made the mistake of getting too close and Hcur smashed his shield into the general. He was stunned and could do nothing about the mace which once again sent him sprawling, one final blow from the bird and Malice never stood again.

Magnus's frustration with Pravus boiled over and in his wrath his guard slipped. Pravus slender sword held by another man would stand no hope against the lion, but in the sorcerer's grasp and with his dark magic's it was thrust into Magnus's side. The blade went in deep, the lion let out a roar so loud almost all in the battle stopped for a moment. From underneath Pravus's dark hood a flash of a grin may have been seen, his cackle was certainly heard by those nearby. The lion king fell.

Braydon with Guardian's sword in hand flew at Pravus, but like Magnus, he could not force the dark wizard back, his defence to the strikes seemed effortless. Braydon, skilled as he was, wasn't the warrior that Magnus was with a sword, his duel with the dark lord was even shorter. Pravus's weapon caught him above his breast plate near his collar bone, its blood stained tip speared right through Braydon emerging the other side. He held Braydon there for a moment, the archer's face was contorted with pain, Pravus studied it with his milky eyes then withdrew the blade. Braydon dropped to his knees Custos Ferrum slipped from his grasp and the prince of Acerbus quickly brought his own blade down on the man's neck.

Austin could only watch in horror while this happened. The battle continued around him like it was taking place in slow motion. He called out Braydon's name as Pravus delivered the fatal blow. Then calmness took him. Austin looked around and saw his friends fighting valiantly, even though many cats and men had now joined the countless Goblyn's in the dirt. He looked over at Pravus standing over his friend's fallen body and he saw the Guardian's sword lying next to it. He went to it slowly it seemed, the dark wizard saw him approach with an amused look he made no attempt to stop the boy.

'I've defeated Magnus, I've defeated your champion and sword bearer, now you, a whelp, dare challenge me.' He laughed as Austin picked up the Phoenix's finest work. Austin held the silver close and looked at it, not a mark from all the fighting no trace of Goblyn blood remained on it.

'Raise it then,' rasped Pravus, 'and join them.' He nodded at Braydon and Magnus. Austin pointed the blade at the dark one who swung at it, Austin's arm barely moved and the blow was blocked. Pravus swung again to the boy's side this time, Austin's arm seemed to move slowly to his side but the blow was parried with time to spare. More strikes were easily dealt with and confusion spread across Pravus's face.

'How is this possible?' but Austin didn't answer instead he let the sword answer for him. Austin thrust at his foe now, a low swing that seemed to take several seconds to deliver but the evil sorcerer stumbled backwards in an attempt to block it.

'What is this witchcraft?' he hissed, 'no one is as powerful as I,' again Austin gave no answer concentring instead on his sword; it gave him total confidence almost like it was guiding him. He swung the silver blade as hard and fast as he could but it still seemed ponderous, Pravus, though, was shaken, unable to comprehend what was happening. Another hard strike and the dark prince was disarmed, his weapon knocked out of reach, in his desperation he lunged at Austin who plunged the Phoenix sword into his heart. The blade disappeared into the black robes, swallowed almost to the hilt, but as long as the sword was it did not exit Pravus back. It almost seemed like it was in a void. Austin held it there and met the astounded gaze of his enemy; words failed the dark wizard now and his eyes grew even paler. Around them everything had stopped, men the cats and even the Goblyn's they all looked on wondering what would happen next, and in what direction this would take the battle.

Austin was finally compelled to withdraw the sword from his foe, as he did so the charcoal robes dropped lifelessly to the floor along with the small silver crown and the thin belt. No flesh no bones were there. Thunder roared in the air though there was not a cloud in the sky, and for a moment everything went black. But only for a moment; the dark storm was now lifted from the land. Austin dropped to his knees exhausted, everything around him that had been happening slowly returned to normal. He was vaguely aware of the Goblyn's fleeing. Hcur would later tell him thousands of them all ran in any direction they could, simple-minded creatures as they were they lost all hope, they panicked at the loss of Malice, they fled without Sinister.

Cheers and songs broke out among the men of Aurum, but Austin was only half aware of it. Hcur arrived and placed his hand on his shoulder, then ruffled his hair. Austin turned to look up, he tried to smile but his muscles failed him. The hawk reached out his hand which Austin took and allowed himself to be dragged up. Jak reached them she dropped her weapons by his feet and gave him a big embrace, and then she wrapped his fingers around the Guardian's sword and pushed it gently to his chest.

'We did it!' she cried. He nodded tears welling up. Hcur hoisted him up straight now.

'Kings don't slouch, lad,' he said, and Austin was now aware the chanting had stopped and all eyes were upon him.

'Hail King Austin son of Arian, son of Argentum, the wizard slayer and king of Rigdedale,' shouted a bloodied Wentwood from nearby. He dropped to one knee and held the sword of the moon up high. In almost one motion all the men in sight dropped to one knee also and raised whatever arms they bore, or just held their hands up in salute.

'Hail King Austin, Hail king Austin.' The cry rang through the air for a long time. Too long for Austin's liking.

'Raise the sword,' whispered Hcur. Sheepishly, Austin did and loud cheers broke out along with applause followed by more hails.

Chapter XIV: A New Beginning

Civitas Aurum was a very busy place in the two weeks after the battle, and it would be for the coming months. It was Austin's coronation day; he felt it was rushed but it was here all the same. He was glad Hcur and Sir Wentwood were around to advise him otherwise he would have been lost. His very first act as king was to bury the fallen; that had been an easy decision, not hard to make, but hard to deal with. So many lives had been lost. Two areas of the plains of Luca had been set aside. One was for their own just about northwest of the city, they were buried a metre apart and an acorn tree was planted with them. Braydon was closest grave to Aurum and given an oak. Next to him with the cats' blessing was Magnus with a great redwood. It wood became known as the golden wood, and there would be a silver wood near Argentum, the trees would be silver birch, and a stone wood near the Ridgegate for the men lost there. A huge ditch was excavated on the plains south of the city, the Goblyn's their limbs weapons boots anything to do with them was piled in. Then it was torched the pyre raged for three nights until the dirt was thrown back over. From that time on it became known as the hill of woe.

He then had to supervise and agree to the rebuilding of the city, deal with the Goblyn threat still at large in the kingdom and a hundred other tasks had come his way. All this while his own grief was still raw. He had sent as many men as could be spared to Argentum, and Jak went with them as Austin was refused permission to go while the Goblyn's still roamed. I've killed Pravus, he thought to himself, I'm king now and they tell me I can't go somewhere because it's dangerous, he shook his head.

Most of the cats returned to Crosstree rock for the time being to deal with their own grief, a confrontation with the birds was prevented when it learned that Apollo had fallen in battle. The creature that slew him was never able to brag though, ripped apart by the other winged warriors. The cats had offered their apologies and condolences and then their assistance to the birds who just wanted to return to the canyon to bury Apollo, the only bird whose life was lost. They were given a tower in the golden castle to live in until they chose a new home, Austin said they could have any pick of the towers and as the towers where named after the nine largest rivers in the land they decided on the Goodyson tower. Hcur was devastated by Apollo's death but stayed by Austin's side; they shared a silent grief together.

'How am I going to cope, old friend?' he asked the hawk.

'He who would learn to fly one day must first learn to stand and walk run and climb and dance.'

'Hcur what does that mean?' Austin laughed before Wentwood answered.

'I think he means take things one step at a time and you'll grow into your role,' the Hawk nodded.

'You would make a better king than me with all your wisdom,' added Austin.

'Apollo once told me, "I am strong because I've been weak. I am fearless because I've been afraid. I am wise because I've been foolish." He looked at the boy. 'You will make a great king. You have the spirit of the Phoenix in you, it guided you to victory in battle and it will guide you in the future I'm certain.'

'Agreed our nation will prosper once more,' the knight said with a satisfied look.

'The great cats the birds and men all equals,' continued Hcur 'and Custos Ferrum to light the way we will have a very bright future indeed.' Austin liked the idea and he guessed he better get used to being king. There must be worse jobs he supposed, now to think of a suitable role for Hcur, an advisor just doesn't cut it.

A few days earlier in a little port far north a couple quietly rode into town. Redpike was the most northerly point in the kingdom the fishing was great and the ships sailed regularly to trade goods with the Miressa isles. The town was always busy though not frantic, the men here had their own pace. Leuan and Catalina had booked passage to Ba'el largest of the Miressa's in terms of commerce though smallest in size. It would be a place where they could plot there next move without prying eyes upon them. Leuan had decided to keep a low profile unsure of his position under a new king. He had learned of course of Austin's victory the whole nation had by now. He still seethed at the idea. He was grateful for Catalina's company, though her usefulness had lessoned somewhat. Most of her agents had been killed in the war, those who hadn't no longer responded to her. Except here in Redpike where her source arranged the passage. Leuan hated the notion of leaving his nation but with the remains of the army scouring the countryside hunting Goblyn's he decided to pack his bags rather than be caught and dragged before the king. Catalina suggested Austin wouldn't do that, that he would let Leuan be, but he would bring in Austin if the roles were reversed so he wouldn't change his mind, and passage was booked.

Just as Leuan under a thick brown cloak and hood was boarding a tall galleon, a deafening whip crack sounded in the air. All looked up expecting to see lightning but it was a beautiful clear sunny day, many of the sailors murmured together old navel rumours about bad omens before sailing.

Catalina turned and noticed Leuan who was still looking up into the heavens.

'Is something the matter, your grace?' she asked. Leuan lowered his head and stared right through her. A cold and evil stare, she noticed his green eyes were now almost ivory.

'Nothing at all,' he hissed.